WHAT YOU SEE IN THE STARS

SOPHIE HAYDON

BAY BOOKS

What You See in the Stars
by Sophie Haydon

A nerdy astronomer. A macho cowboy. And a heartache that neither could have seen in the stars...

—The Mackenzies—
A Place Called Home
Secrets at Parata Bay
Escape to Shelter Springs
What you See in the Stars
Second Chance at Whisper Creek
Summer at the Lakehouse Café

—Lantern Bay—
Yours to Give
Yours to Treasure
Yours to Cherish
Yours to Keep
Yours Forever
Yours to Love

For more information about this author, visit:
https://sophiehaydon.com

ISBN 978-199-102108-3 (Amazon Print)
ISBN 978-199-102127-4 (Draft2Digital Print)
© 2015 Diana Fraser

CONTENTS

PROLOGUE

Even seen through the driving rain, the colonial mansion of Glencoe was impressive—grander than Morgan West had imagined. Framed by dark trees, it stood large and imposing beyond a lake, its reflection fragmented by the rain.

"They expecting you, mate?" asked the stranger from whom he'd hitched a lift.

Morgan tipped up his hat from which rain had already started to drip and whistled his dog, Annie, to heel. She was always curious, keen to check things out before her master, to make sure he was safe. It was almost as if she knew there was no one else to do it.

"Yeah, they're expecting me. Thanks for the lift."

"Any time."

He slammed the door closed and the ute roared off back up the track to the cluster of estate cottages that lay some distance from the homestead. Morgan had been lucky to bump into the man in the pub. It had saved him a long walk in the rain. Not that he'd have minded. He was used to being out in all weather.

He slung his duffel bag over his shoulder and walked around the lake, and up the tree-lined drive. By the time he arrived at the sweep of steps that led up to the large double doors, he and Annie were soaked. Luckily, it was still summer—and the January rains were welcome in the usually dry high country of New Zealand's South Island.

He lifted the hefty brass knocker and brought it sharply down three times. Then he waited. There was no response. He knocked once more. This time a light turned on inside and he heard a woman's shrill voice call out, followed by the distant sound of sharp heels on a wooden floor. Then a further call, then nothing.

He was about to raise the knocker once more, when the door opened suddenly. A woman stood there, past sixty, upright and slender with white hair immaculately secured in a bun, dressed in a tweed skirt and pale blue sweater with a string of pearls around her neck.

"Yes." She peered at him. "What do you want?"

The arrogance, the rudeness, it was all as his mother had described. He could see she'd been very beautiful once. If it hadn't been for her sour expression she'd be beautiful still.

"I said"—her eyes narrowed with anger—"what do you want?"

"I'm here for the job. It's been arranged with Callum Mackenzie."

"*Mr* Mackenzie to you. The workers' cottages and dormitories are over there. What were you thinking coming to the front door?" She pointed but he didn't look in the direction to which she pointed. Instead, he noticed her hands—slender and white, untouched by the ravages of hard work that had marked his dead mother's hands.

What was he thinking, indeed? But it had been no

mistake. When he'd seen the piece in the paper about the forthcoming settlement of the Mackenzie lands, he knew he'd have to come. It had reminded him of all the stories he'd listened to over the years about this place and this woman. He'd decided it was time to see them both.

"Sorry to have bothered you, ma'am." He tipped his hat. She appeared satisfied by the gesture, deaf to the heavy sarcasm in his tone. The door slammed shut before he'd turned away.

He smiled grimly to himself as he walked back into the pouring rain and along the path that led to the workers' cottages.

Now he'd seen the house and Lady Mackenzie, should he turn around and walk back into the rainy night and keep on walking, like he'd been doing for half his life? No, not yet. He'd told the manager he'd work for a season and he'd never reneged on his word.

Besides, it would give him more time to see what life might have been like if things had been different...

CHAPTER ONE

Fifteen months later...

"Hi!" Rebecca Mayhew greeted Callum Mackenzie as she wove her way through the crowds of people who'd come to the Lakehouse Café to see her friend Gemma's paintings.

Callum returned the greeting but Rebecca kept walking, not wanting to engage in conversation. Callum and Gemma's relationship was going through a difficult patch and she hadn't a clue what to say to her best friend's husband. Give Rebecca a computer and a mathematical problem to solve and she'd get a result. But ask her to fathom the ins and outs of a relationship and she drew a blank every time. She smiled encouragingly at Callum and hoped that would be enough.

Then her gaze shifted to the handsome man beside him who had a look of open admiration on his face. A low whistle escaped lips that quirked into a smile. That must be Callum's younger brother, James, whom she'd heard so much about. She looked behind her, wondering who he was looking at, shrugged and continued on her way toward a very pregnant Gemma who was resting on a stool. She passed Gemma one of the two long glasses of herb tea she was carrying.

"It looks like it's going well, Gem."

Gemma took a sip of her tea. "Much better than I imagined. I've sold out."

Rebecca looked around at Gemma's paintings—abstracts mainly, inspired by the Mackenzie Country—which hung on every available wall space. "I'm not surprised. They're fantastic."

"There's even talk of an exhibition in Christchurch."

"Well..." Rebecca hesitated, wondering why her friend looked so unhappy. "Isn't that good news? You have enough material, right?"

Gemma gave a brief smile. "Yeah, of course."

"Then what's the problem?"

Gemma glanced through the crowd at Callum. "Nothing I can't sort out."

"Good. It's about time. Not that I don't like you staying at my place. It's lovely. You're the sister I never had."

Gemma slipped her arm around her friend and gave her a hug. "Me too." Then she burst into giggles on Rebecca's shoulder.

"What?"

"It's Morgan. He's here again. He was just looking over at you. He's turned away now. Strange how he appears wherever you are. The only time I've ever seen him at the café is when you're here. Funny that."

"Shelter Springs is a small place." But Rebecca frowned. She hadn't thought it strange before but come to think of it, whenever she was away from the Mount John Observatory, she'd often catch sight of his dog first, go to pet her and then Morgan would appear. "I often see him around town. Not so surprising really, is it?"

"I know for a fact that the only time Morgan isn't at Glencoe working his butt off is when he comes into town at a certain time every day. And who else's schedule is as regular as clockwork?"

"Mine. Well, we have something in common then."

Gemma sighed, exasperated. "He only comes in to town because he knows he's going to see you heading to your stint in the Information Center."

"I doubt it. It's a long way to come just to nod at me, look uncomfortable and then disappear again."

"Callum told me that Morgan won't accept a permanent position but that he doesn't seem in any hurry to leave either." Gemma looked slyly at Rebecca. "I wonder why?"

Rebecca shrugged. "Because he likes it here?"

They both looked over to where Glencoe's mysterious farm hand stood propped against the bar with a beer in his hand. He caught their eye, took a hasty swig and suddenly became absorbed in looking at one particular painting.

"He's just looking at your paintings."

Gemma sighed. "Oh, Becks, face it, you have an admirer, whether you want one or not."

"I don't mind having an admirer, so long as he's the right *sort* of admirer."

"The right sort. Okay, by that I take it you mean the kind of guy you've described on your list."

"You've seen my list?"

"I'm sorry, but your notebook was lying there one day and I thought it was mine."

"So you opened it and discovered my checklist for a husband."

Gemma grinned and nodded. "I didn't think people really did that."

"Well *I* do. And I don't see what's so strange about it. If you're buying a house you'd make a list of the things you want."

"That's a house. Not a man."

"I don't see the difference."

"It *is* a long time since you've been out with someone," laughed Gemma.

"Maybe. Anyway, my point is that Morgan West is hardly the sort of man who'd be on my list."

"Why not?"

"For one thing no one knows anything about him. He appeared out of nowhere and will probably disappear with equal swiftness. You can't trust people like that."

"Why not? That's the way some people like it."

"Maybe. But it's not how *I* like it."

Gemma shrugged. "You have to admit he's built, though. Just like Callum is."

Rebecca looked over at him. The mysterious Morgan West had his back to them. Even in the chill of the winter, Morgan was wearing only a faded shirt that hung from broad shoulders. He held the hat he usually wore in his hands, having raked back his golden curly hair off his face. It was too long—just like everything about Morgan West was "too" something.

"He's certainly tall... And broad..."—she frowned—"and his shoulders are very wide." She swallowed. "And I've never seen such large biceps before. They're, well, they're very... I don't know what they are. They kind of make you want to touch them."

Gemma followed her gaze. "I guess your astronomer colleagues don't have the muscles country men have." She looked at Callum who was making his way over to Morgan. "Like Callum. I think he had me from the first moment I saw his shirtsleeves rolled up. There's something about a man who you know could physically manhandle you if you wanted him to." She shook her head as she tried to re-focus.

Rebecca, too, sucked in a long calming breath. The thought of being manhandled—in the right way—by someone so much bigger and taller than her did strange things to her. "But... *but*," she repeated more firmly, "muscles aren't everything."

"Aren't they?" asked Gemma dreamily, her gaze still firmly on her husband.

"No, they're not. Morgan hardly spoke to me at your hen night."

"I don't think a party is his natural habitat. And *you* have to take some of the responsibility for that. *You* hardly said a word to him either."

"True. Parties aren't my natural habitat either."

"Why don't you go and speak to him now?"

"No, he's probably quite happy looking at the paintings."

"Rebecca! He's here to see *you*."

"Do you really think so?"

"I *know* so. *You* don't notice these things. But *I* do. Now, for goodness sake, put him out of his misery and go and say hello to him."

Despite herself, she was tempted. There was something in the way his too-long hair fell over that collar...and those muscles... She sighed. "Then what?"

"Follow your instincts."

"Instincts? Hm..." Following her instincts wasn't something Rebecca could ever remember doing.

"Besides, why not have some fun with Morgan?"

"No," said Rebecca indignantly. "I'm not having fun. I'm just going over to be friendly, to be polite."

"Why? You're not going out with your astronomer colleague, Martin, are you? He's not here, is he?"

Rebecca went to push her glasses further on her nose from force of habit before she remembered that Gemma had persuaded her to replace them with contact lenses. "No. He's at the observatory, but... it doesn't seem right."

"Don't tell me. He scores highly on your husband list."

"As a matter of fact, he does."

Gemma sighed. "So, tell me what it is this Martin, whom I've never yet met, has that the ruggedly handsome Morgan doesn't."

Rebecca shrugged. "I can't say exactly." She glanced back at Morgan who was now talking to Callum. "I just know who I am when I'm with someone like Martin. But with Morgan..." She trailed off unable to explain how out of her depth she felt whenever he was near.

Gemma frowns. "Who you *are*? Don't you know?" She narrowed her eyes. "Is this something to do with you being adopted?"

Rebecca waved her hand in confusion. Even if she could figure it all out herself, now wasn't the time for deep soul-searching. "Probably," she replied. "Anyway, Martin is reliable, he has a good sense of humor, and is good looking in a neat sort of way—"

Gemma held up her hand. "Stop right there! 'A neat sort of way'? That's it." She gave Rebecca a little shove. "You need to get over there and have a close encounter with someone who's good looking in a muscly sort of way. And if that's not enough for you, check Morgan against your list. If he doesn't measure up, then tell him you're not interested."

"You think?"

"It's the only kind thing to do. He fancies you rotten and for some reason he can't bring himself to make a move. So it's up to you to sort it out. Once and for all."

Rebecca jumped off the stool and tugged her cardigan back into place. "Okay. I don't believe he fancies me rotten, but if he does, it's best that I don't lead him on. Best I nip it in the bud before it becomes something more than it is."

"Go," grinned Gemma.

"Right." She smiled wanly back and stepped forward into the crowd before she could give herself time to think.

She walked up behind him and looked up. She felt tiny. Close to, she could plainly see the bulge and swell of his muscles under his much-washed shirt—the checked material was thin in places. Then he lifted his beer bottle and his rolled-up shirtsleeve revealed a heavily tanned arm, sprinkled with blond hair and those muscles again. Gemma was right. At close quarters they had an even greater effect on her. She squeezed her hands tight, as her desire to reach out and touch them, to run her fingers over their shape and strength, became almost overwhelming. She swallowed. This was ridiculous. She had nothing to say to him. She'd leave. Just at that moment Callum caught sight of her.

"Rebecca! Come and keep Morgan company while I go see Gemma."

Morgan swung around as if startled and there they were, pushed close to each other by the jostling crowd. And all Rebecca could think of was that she wanted to bury her nose in his chest and smell him. She shook her head, trying to quieten her beating heart.

"Hello again," she said, wondering whether shaking hands would satisfy her need to touch him. She extended her hand but he made no move to take it, so she let it drop.

Morgan nodded in greeting and made some kind of grunt.

She'd have looked around for inspiration for something to say if her eyes weren't level with his open shirt where she could see an equally tanned chest sprinkled with blond hairs. She felt the heat of a blush rise from somewhere deep within, warming her stomach, her neck and her cheeks. She never blushed. She took a deep breath and looked up and... wished she hadn't. If she'd hoped that making eye contact would loosen her tongue, she'd been wrong. From a distance his eyes were usually narrowed. But here, so close, she could see they were a vivid blue. A beautiful baby blue that was accentuated by his tanned skin and was at odds with his rugged cowboy appearance.

"Oh," she breathed.

He frowned. "Are you okay?"

She nodded. "Sure."

"Like a drink?"

"Yes, please."

"Tea?"

She needed something stronger than that. "A glass of white wine."

He leaned through the crowds and plucked a glass off the tray from a passing waitress and handed it to her.

"Thank you." She took a sip and another deep breath. This was going to be harder than she thought. "So... you're here to see the paintings?"

"No."

"Oh."

"I've seen most of them in Gemma's studio at Glencoe," he said.

"Oh yes. Of course."

"I suppose you've seen the paintings already, too."

She nodded. "Yes, but I wouldn't have missed this for the world. A big day for Gemma."

"I guess," he muttered.

"But you're not here for Gemma," she said.

"Not really."

"Then... why?"

"I thought *you'd* be here."

She should have guessed that, as a man of so few words, when he did finally speak he'd be totally direct. "Oh. Well, you were right. I'm here. So, did you want to tell me something?"

"No."

"Then why did you want to see me?" She took a hasty sip of wine.

He hesitated, glanced around as if looking for help, and returned his gaze to her and sighed. "I think you're beautiful."

She spluttered and choked on the wine. Morgan took her wine glass from her and patted her rather too firmly on the back as she continued to cough.

"You okay?"

"I suppose." She took back the wine glass from Morgan. "You don't beat about the bush when it comes to saying what you think, do you?"

"I'm not into making noise for the sake of it. No point."

"I guess you're right. So... you think I'm beautiful." She felt the color flood her cheeks again, but she didn't care. She couldn't remember anyone ever calling her beautiful before, except maybe her father when she was little, and that didn't count.

"Yes. You are." A flicker of a grin creased at the corners of his mouth. "In every way."

"Really?"

"Yeah. I can't stop looking at you. I guess you've noticed."

"Well." She shrugged, then laughed. "It's been drawn to my attention."

"Do you mind?"

She thought for a moment. She should mind. She'd come over to Morgan to let him down gently, to tell him she wasn't the woman for him. "No," she heard herself saying. And it was true. She didn't. In fact, she positively liked the thought of him looking at her. The thought drove flutterings deep inside her. "No, I don't."

His eyes narrowed sexily and there was a corresponding jolt of pure lust which made her gasp. She swayed toward him and he stepped a little closer as if to meet her half way. He was so close now, as people mingled all around them, that she could smell the freshly laundered smell of his shirt, and something more... something mouth-wateringly male.

There was a whoop of laughter close by and the noise level rose. He dipped his head toward her. "Good," he whispered in her ear. His breath warmed her neck and lower. It was all she could do to stop herself from pulling his head to hers so she could feel his breath against her mouth, in her mouth. But he withdrew and looked at her through eyes that, despite their narrowed gaze, seemed to look deep inside of her. And goodness only knew what he'd see there. She didn't want him to see into the place where she was vulnerable, to the place where she didn't even allow herself to look.

She stepped away. "But, oh"—she looked at her watch—"it's time I got going. Night shift at the Observatory, you know. It's where I work."

He nodded. "I know. You're a star-gazer."

"Oh, no. We don't just gaze at stars. It's very scientific.

My project involves constructing theoretical models to show that the link between star formation and molecular clouds results from the correlation between chemical phase, shielding, and temperature." She paused, wondering if she'd gotten carried away. In her enthusiasm for the subject, she often did. "It's cutting edge stuff."

He smiled. "I'm sure."

"Do you, er, like stars?"

"Sure. As a kid I spent a lot of time looking at them. I used to make shapes of them."

"What kind of shapes did you make?"

"*Taniwhas*, mainly. Maori monsters," he elaborated, obviously thinking she wouldn't know what they were.

"Oh," Rebecca said, unable to prevent a certain disappointment. Because she also liked to make shapes from the stars—the geometric kind—and not one had ever been a *taniwha*. She sighed. "Anyway, I need to go. I'll find Gemma and..." She looked around in vain. "Where is she?"

"You don't have a lift home?"

"No. But that's fine. It's not far. I'll walk."

"I'll drive you home."

"Really, I don't want to put you to any bother."

"It's no bother. Though I came with Callum so I'll get his keys." He looked around. "Looks like he's gone too. I'll walk you home instead."

"I don't want to put you out."

"You won't be. Remember, I'm here to look at you and I can do that for a little while longer if I walk you home."

"I guess you can. But it's a bit stalkerish, isn't it?"

He frowned. "What? Me walking you home?"

"No, you wanting to look at me."

"I don't mean it in a weird way. I guess I'm saying I find

you very attractive and I'd like to spend time with you. Does that sound less stalkerish?"

"Yes. That's much better."

"So, can I take you home?"

She glanced around for Gemma but couldn't see her and turned back to Morgan and smiled. "Yes, that would be very nice. Thank you."

Morgan took a step forward and the crowd seemed to part before him. He unhooked his coat from the old fashioned coat stand by the door. "Where's your coat?"

She grimaced. "In Gemma's car."

"Here, take this. Really. I don't feel the cold."

She shouldn't have, but for some reason she let him slip his coat around her shoulders. They walked out onto the road in silence. Rebecca looked around. "I wonder where Gemma's gone. I really should say goodbye to her.

Morgan nodded toward Shelter lake where a couple stood under a lamp post. "Might be a good idea to give her and Callum a bit of space."

"Oh, right! Hm! About time they sorted out their differences."

They both looked at Callum and Gemma just as they kissed. "Looks like they've done that all right." He looked at Rebecca and she could have sworn his gaze dropped to her lips. She licked them and he looked back into her eyes. "Here"—he held out his coat so she could slip her arms into the sleeves—"put the coat on properly. You'll freeze."

"Are you sure you don't mind?"

"Nah, I'm fine."

"Well, if you're sure," she said, noticing that snow was beginning to fall. "It's not far."

They fell into step, Morgan slowing his to match her smaller strides.

"How often do you work nights?"

Thank goodness. A normal question which didn't involve her either fantasizing about his body or racking her brains for what to say next. "Just a couple of nights a week. My main job is at the computer. I also do some community education work in town for tourists."

"Wednesdays. When you go to the Tourist Information office."

"Yes." Gemma was right. He *had* been following her. It didn't pay to think about. It made her feel dizzy. "But I miss being at the telescope. You can see everything then."

"Must be magic."

They turned the corner and her small cottage was up ahead. "Magic?" She shrugged under his massive jacket. "I don't know about that. Fascinating though."

She stopped at her picket fence and followed his gaze up to the starry sky.

"Looks pretty magical to me. Makes you believe in things you shouldn't."

She frowned. "I don't usually star gaze without the telescope. Not much point."

"Do you need a point to do things? Sure, they've helped me find my way around the bush at night but sometimes I just look at them because they're just so damn pretty."

It was her turn to smile. He was full of surprises. "Seems to be a habit of yours, looking at pretty things."

She faltered then, as she realized she'd just called herself "pretty". Not something she was in the habit of doing. Slowly he looked down at her. "All I do is look, sweetheart. No need to worry."

"I wasn't." She looked away, embarrassed. "Worrying, I mean."

He nodded. "Goodnight, then." His face was shadowed

from the street lamp by his hat. But as he turned she caught sight of the line of his jaw, strong and determined.

"Goodnight," she called out but he was already walking away. She didn't want him to leave like that. Not without knowing how she was feeling. "Morgan!"

He stopped and slowly turned around. He didn't say anything, just waited for her to speak again.

She went running up to him, slipped out of his coat and handed it to him. "Thank you. For the coat. For the walk home."

"You're welcome."

"And... if you wanted to, you know, come and look at me again, some time, that would be fine."

He grinned. "It sure would."

He walked away, his footsteps muffled on the slowly accumulating snow. She waited until he turned the corner and then suddenly aware of the shivers that were beginning to course uncontrollably through her, returned to her gate and walked up the short path to her front door.

Before she went inside she glanced upward. The stars that people came from all over the world to see in the Mackenzie Country's dark sky were indecently bright and abundant. And for a moment she looked at them through Morgan's eyes and they became mysterious, unfathomable, and magical. But then she spotted the pulsating red giant star of Mira and she made a mental note to catch up on the latest research paper on the pulsations and shock waves produced by low mass supergiant stars.

She went inside the small cottage, still warm from the damped down fire. She briefly paused as she passed the spare room where Gemma had been staying. It looked like she wouldn't be back tonight. *And* would no doubt be moving back to Glencoe. It hadn't been easy for either

Gemma or Callum but Rebecca was glad they'd made it up. Not just for the baby's sake but for their own. She knew they loved each other. But she also knew the course of love rarely ran smoothly.

She walked into her bedroom, set down her bag and opened her notebook to the page at the back, where her list was.

For years she'd been so focused on her studies and work that she hadn't wanted a serious relationship. But Gemma's pregnancy had stirred Rebecca's own maternal instincts and she'd done what she always did in response to a problem—made a list.

She glanced through the ten points that she required of a potential mate.

1. *Self-confident (but not arrogant)*
2. *Respectful of women and feminists*
3. *Good career*
4. *Careful with money*
5. *Tall (but not too tall)*
6. *Steady and responsible*
7. *Well-traveled*
8. *Good conversationalist*
9. *Well-educated*
10. *Of neat build (not too slim and not too broad)*

All reasonable, or necessary. She wanted someone who would fit in. Someone much like herself. Except taller of course. But not too tall. A logical list. If only people had a more scientific approach she was sure there would be fewer separations, fewer unhappy marriages like her own parents who still lived separate lives in their terraced house in

Manchester. No, her list was the only rational approach to finding a husband.

Suddenly the line of Morgan's jaw, lit by the streetlamp, filled her mind, giving her stomach a little flip of desire. This was swiftly followed by her memory of his back, the soft, well-worn shirt pulled across his broad shoulders as he reached over to pick up a beer. And those muscles.

She swallowed. And doodled beside point 10. She hesitated only a moment before crossing it out. Adding 'Strong physique' instead. She'd simply got it wrong. Hadn't considered it sufficiently. Now she'd seen the kind of physique she liked, she could alter her requirements.

Nothing was ever set in stone, after all. Maybe there was room in her life for someone a little different to the man on her list. Maybe she should tweak her list a little over the next few weeks. It's what scientists did with a good hypothesis. Nothing wrong with that.

She was sweet, Morgan thought as he walked back to the café. Sweet and way out of his league. Still, as he'd told her, he was just looking, just passing the time of day with her. Nothing more. He'd be moving on in a few months. Just as he always did. Didn't mean he couldn't appreciate her company from time to time.

He smiled as he remembered the way she spoke. There was no pretense about her like there was with other women. She meant what she said—direct. But it also made her vulnerable. He stopped walking and frowned. He didn't like to think of her as vulnerable.

"What's up, mate?"

He turned to see Callum leaning against the lamppost, alone now. "Nothing. Ready to go?"

Callum shook his head. "I'm waiting for Gemma. She's coming back with us to Glencoe."

"Good. I'm pleased for you. She's a good woman."

Callum grinned. "High praise from you." He paused. "Thanks for staying on to fill the manager's role. Are you sure you won't take on the role long term?"

"No. I'll be moving on as soon as you get someone to replace me."

"Where to?"

Morgan shrugged. "Just on. Something always turns up."

Callum shook his head. "Always moving, eh?"

"It's the way I like it."

"Fair enough. Would you mind driving the truck home?"

"Sure, no problem."

Callum tossed Morgan the keys and pushed himself off the post and walked to the café door as Gemma stepped out. "See you later. Tomorrow." He grinned and greeted Gemma with a lingering kiss.

Morgan turned away abruptly, opened the door of the Glencoe truck and jumped in. He revved the engine, drowning out the laughter of the happy couple as they lingered in the falling snow.

Yeah, he'd be moving on... just as he always did.

CHAPTER TWO

The snow-capped mountains looked pristine against a bright blue sky as Rebecca drove along the road which led to Glencoe. Gemma didn't know she was coming. It was a spur of the moment decision. A basket of presents for the baby from Rebecca's co-workers at the observatory was excuse enough.

Then her phone went and she glanced at it. It was a text from Gemma. Rebecca picked it up and, with half an eye on the empty road, quickly read it. Gemma was in town and wondered if they could catch up.

Rebecca felt only a momentary pang of guilt before tossing the phone back onto the seat without answering. Instead, she gripped the wheel and focused on where she was going. If she'd answered, Gemma would wonder why she hadn't turned back to meet her. So... she wouldn't answer. Because Gemma was only an excuse. As much as she loved her best friend, it wasn't Gemma she was going to see.

Rebecca drove carefully around some of the sheltered bends, the ice still lying in shadowy pockets, untouched by the low sun. She drove past the lake and the place where she usually parked and pulled up instead outside the art studio where she knew Morgan would be working. And where Gemma might have been, if she'd been at Glencoe.

Gemma had told her that Morgan was extending her art studio. As the months had gone by with Morgan working at Glencoe, Callum had increasingly come to rely on him as his right-hand man, despite his lack of permanence. But apparently Morgan hadn't exactly relished office duties and, when the opportunity arose to get his hands dirty with some building work, he'd grabbed it.

Rebecca got out of the car and heard the tell-tale sound of hammer on wallboard and knew it was him. She slammed the door but the rhythm didn't pause. She smiled to herself. Just like him. Concentrating on what he was doing and not about to stop out of curiosity. Besides, she realized, he wouldn't imagine for one moment that the visitor would be for him.

She'd waited long enough for him to phone her. He hadn't. So it was up to her. But she hated phones. Never knew what to say. So here she was... holding a basket of baby clothes.

She walked up and opened the doors and stepped inside. She was immediately assailed by the smell of fresh sawdust and the heat coming from the potbelly stove. She couldn't see him but she could hear him though. Clutching the basket of presents, she walked further into the studio. The sound was coming from beyond a partition. She paused to look at some of Gemma's recent work. Her artwork was changing, developing, more settled somehow. She'd obviously been painting a lot, knowing she wouldn't be getting so much time after the baby had arrived. Gemma's baby was already overdue.

Then she laughed. She walked towards a painting and saw it was of her, frowning slightly as she stared with unerring focus at the painter. Gemma had caught her "intense" look as Gemma called it, to a T.

She was suddenly aware the sound had stopped. Not so much by the cessation of sound but by a little shiver that ran up her body. She turned to see Morgan appear from behind the partition. He was clad only in jeans, no shirt, and his body was slick with sweat.

"It's you," he said, with characteristic brevity.

She swallowed. All memory of the little speech she'd prepared vanished. He stood there like a god. From his broad shoulders and strong arms—on which the golden sunlight shone, highlighting the contours of his muscles—to the dark gold hair that trailed into old jeans sitting low on his hips. She looked up abruptly, suddenly aware of where her gaze had lingered. "Yes, it's me," she answered, her voice strangely husky. She cleared her throat. "I've come to..."

Morgan tossed the hammer onto the work bench with a clang and took a step towards her. It wasn't much, but it was enough to make her unable to finish her sentence. She didn't move—she couldn't move—as he walked up to her, his eyes searching her face. He stopped in front of her, too close. Sawdust covered his chest and the chiseled muscles on his stomach in a dusting of pale gold. His muscles, pumped by the recent activity, gleamed with fresh sweat of which she instinctively took a deep breath.

She looked up into his eyes. "Hello," she managed to croak from between dry lips. She licked them and noticed his gaze flicker briefly to her mouth.

A whisper of a smile briefly lit his face. "Hello."

The seconds lengthened until it turned into a silence which neither of them seemed in a hurry to break. Rebecca's head was usually full of thoughts, full of words and facts and figures but now, for some reason, only one fact floated into her mind and stayed there—for all Morgan's strength and hard muscles, his lips curved with a sensual flare when he was amused. And apparently he was now amused.

"If you're looking for Gemma," the beautiful lips said, "she's not here."

She glanced back to his eyes. "I know."

"You didn't come to see Gemma?"

She shook her head. She'd never been able to say anything other than the truth, whatever the potential consequences might be.

He frowned. "So..." He raised his hand and brought it up to hers. As his fingers wrapped around hers she tensed momentarily and then relaxed as his hand took control and raised hers, still holding the basket. "So..." he repeated, lifting the basket into the air. "These"—he narrowed his eyes as he glanced at its contents—"baby clothes are for me?"

She nodded before she realized what he'd said. Then she looked at what their joined hands were holding. "No!" She blushed and looked up at him startled. For someone who never blushed—not for anything, or anybody, anywhere—she seemed to be doing it a lot recently.

Heat flared in her cheeks, bringing forth a bloom of sweat that had nothing to do with the heat in the room, and everything to do with the semi-naked man in front of her. She stepped back as if he were scorching her. And then turned on her heels and walked over to the art table and put down the basket. "The clothes are for Gemma's baby." She unbuttoned her coat, needing to cool down and regain control before she turned to him.

"She's in Shelter Springs today. You could have saved yourself a journey."

She took a deep breath and turned around. "I wanted to come to Glencoe."

His face creased once more into a frown, an expression which she realized was never far away. The muscles in his face pushed against the scored line between his brows, as if falling into a place with which they were very familiar. "Really?" He glanced at the painting. "Then perhaps you've come to see your portrait?"

"No, I didn't know Gemma was painting one of me." She almost winced, realizing she'd just given away a perfectly good reason for being here. She walked up to it, inspecting it. It was a big painting. It wasn't finished yet. The background had been sketched in. The lower half unfinished. But the top half—with Rebecca's dark hair framing a pale face with eyes that looked at the viewer with an uncanny intensity—surprised her. "I look pretty scary."

Her concentration on the painting faltered as she heard his booted footsteps approach, echoing on the wooden floor. He stood just behind her, looking at the painting over her head. "Scary? That's not how I'd have described it."

"And how would you describe how I look?"

She caught her breath, suddenly realizing just what she'd asked him. She remained resolutely still, unable to turn, too aware of him looming so large and powerful behind her.

"You look... unaware."

She swung around, curiosity getting the better of her, as usual.

"What do you mean, 'unaware'? That's an odd way to describe me."

His eyes slid from the painting to her. "Odd maybe, but

that's as I see it." He pointed at the painting. "You're looking like you do when you look at anything or anyone. You're trying to figure out what makes them tick and yet you're kind of..." He trailed off.

"Unaware?" she helped out.

"Um," he agreed with a grunt.

"I still don't understand what you mean."

He took a few steps back. "Ignore me. I didn't mean anything by it. I don't know, it's just..."

She turned to face him again. "Just what? Tell me. I'd love to know."

He sighed. "It's just... there's nothing between you and the world. No pretense."

"Pretense. No, I guess not. Why bother pretending?"

"Most people do. To protect themselves mainly, I guess."

"Yes, I suppose you're right." She suddenly felt uncomfortable at how deep their conversation had plunged, just within a few sentences. She smiled uncertainly. "Perhaps I should pretend. I might look a little less scary."

He shook his head, his expression serious. "No. Don't do that. There's nothing in that look which can confuse a man. It doesn't hide anything."

"But I've nothing to hide."

"No, you're kind of innocent."

She felt her eyes widen with surprise. "Innocent? I'm twenty-five, I'm hardly innocent."

His frown twitched deeper. "I don't mean that kind of innocence."

"Then what?"

He shrugged and stepped away. "I don't know. I'm no good with words. All I know is that you're the opposite of scary."

"Well... in that case, perhaps you'd offer me a drink?"

He looked surprised. "Sure. There's some coffee, or some kind of tea which I think Gemma keeps out here." He rummaged around looking suddenly uncomfortable. "Here." He held up a box and read the label. "Raspberry leaf?"

She laughed. "No thanks. I think that's to help pregnant women with their contractions."

He dropped the box in embarrassment.

"A coffee will be just fine, thanks."

It was Rebecca's turn to be puzzled as, instead of turning on the state-of-the-art coffee machine which Gemma had installed on her work bench, Morgan opened a half-empty jar of instant coffee and chipped away at the hardened grains with a damp spoon.

She turned away to hide her smile. If he thought she was entirely without guile, what about him? She watched as he spooned in the coffee into a chipped cup for him and one of Gemma's fine bone china cups for her. Why didn't he use one of Gemma's as well?

She walked around the studio, looking at the paintings before coming to a stop before the large sliding windows that looked out over the lake, to the valley and to the snow-capped mountains beyond.

He handed her a cup of unappealing looking coffee.

"Thank you. It's a fantastic spot Gemma has here. She's very lucky."

He looked out at the view. "Yeah, it's a good estate. One of the best."

"You're not from round here though, are you?"

"No."

Rebecca was beginning to realize that making conversation wasn't going to be easy with Morgan. She mentally adjusted point 8 on her wish list. Conversation was so over-rated.

"Where are you from?"

"I grew up on the West Coast."

"Greymouth? Hokitika?" she ventured.

He shook his head. "You won't have heard of it. A small settlement up in the bush." He paused and she didn't fill the silence. "My stepfather was a hunter. There was just my mother and me. So..."

"So?"

He shrugged. "So... it was a quiet life."

"Where did you go to school?"

"I didn't. There was correspondence school but no one bothered me with it. I used to go bush most days. Trapping things, making things. Helped my mother out. Life was pretty basic out there."

"I can't imagine it."

"Best not to. It was a tough life. Not a good one. You're from England?"

She nodded. "Manchester. Then university at Oxford and then here, to New Zealand, on a post-doc. St John's Observatory is the best place in the world to study galaxy formation and evolution. That's my area of research."

He nodded, but he had the glazed look that most people had when she talked of her research.

"How long are you here for?" he asked.

"I've decided to stay." She glanced at her full cup, decided there was no way she was going to drink it and placed it on the bookcase by the window. He'd probably never notice. "I love it here. I bought my house last year. I'll travel between here and Christchurch for meetings and such. Otherwise... I'm here to stay."

He didn't say anything for a few moments, just drank some

of the disgusting lukewarm instant drink that was only distantly related to coffee. He replaced his empty cup and turned to her.

"Why are you here, Rebecca?"

"You said you'd come by to see me. You didn't."

"Didn't reckon you meant it."

"I did! I don't say things I don't mean. I thought you'd realize that after what you've just said."

"Yeah, I should have done. But... well..."

"You doubted yourself."

He nodded.

"You shouldn't. Doubt yourself I mean. I really wanted to see you again. I don't know, last time I saw you"—she frowned as she tried to explain what she'd felt—"I just knew I needed to see you again. And then when I didn't, I kept thinking about you. Wondering what you were doing."

He raised his eyebrows in surprise. "Doing? Working. That's all, just working."

She glanced at his muscles. "That's what I thought. That's what I imagined."

"You imagined me working? What, like this? Without a shirt?"

She bit her lip and then nodded.

"Um..." He stepped toward her. "Turns out you were right. And turns out I was wrong because I didn't imagine you like this." He reached out and lightly touched her arm, covered with a thick jumper, beneath which she wore a t-shirt. His finger curled around one of the chunky swirls of the Aran sweater and sunk it inside the center of the swirl. The feel of his finger against her bare arm sent crazy signals to all parts of her body, cutting off any thought.

With the lightest of touches, he curled his finger around the knot of wool and pulled her to him. And she came. She was at eye level with his bare chest and stayed there, transfixed by the springy hairs, by the sawdust which dappled his shoulders and by the smell of him.

"Rebecca?" His voice rumbled in his body and she felt it in her gut.

"Um?" She didn't raise her face to his, only her palm and placed it against his chest. Lightly at first, feeling the springy hairs tickling against the delicate skin on the inside of her wrist. She sucked in a lungful of air as she pushed her hand firmly against his chest. She felt a corresponding sharp intake of breath with him.

"Rebecca! What are you doing?"

She raised her eyes to his which looked down at her, dark and dangerous. "Touching you. Like I've wanted to do from the minute I got here."

He pressed his hand briefly against hers before dragging it away. "You don't know what you're playing with."

"I think I do." She might be innocent about most things but she knew instinctively what she wanted and what he could give her at this moment. She looked back at his chest and pressed her lips against his skin, kissing him, breathing him in.

He pushed his fingers through hers and gripped them, trying to pull her away. But she wasn't having it. She pressed her cheek against his chest and with her other hand smoothed her fingers over his stomach, her fingertips grazing the top of his jeans. He sucked in a sudden breath, placed one hand under her bottom and lifted her up in one swift movement.

Hot and hungry, his mouth was on hers, his tongue finding hers in a frenzied kiss. She gripped his head with her hands so he couldn't move away. With her legs wrapped around his hips, she was acutely aware of the intimacy of their bodies. But it only made her want more.

She didn't know how long they stood, his hands under her bottom, their mouths locked and her hips, shifting instinctively against him. But suddenly the sound of an insistent ringing filtered into her brain, closely followed by the sound of car doors banging.

He pulled away first, gave her bottom another squeeze and then lowered her reluctantly to the floor. "I'm sorry, Rebecca, I didn't mean—" He broke off and picked up the phone.

Shakily she pushed her fingers through her hair and walked away, only half-listening to his side of the conversation which ended abruptly. She heard the sound of Gemma and Callum laughing outside and knew Gemma would be inside soon, looking for her.

She turned to Morgan who'd clicked off the phone.

"Who was it? Anyone important?"

"No. No one important." She was surprised at the bitter tone of his voice.

"Good." They both glanced toward the sound of approaching footsteps, then looked back at each other. "Do you eat?"

"Of course I eat."

"Good. Because I cook. Well. I cook well. I follow the recipe of course otherwise..." Her mind forgot where it was going as he tugged a shirt on over his muscled and tanned body.

"Because you like to follow the rules."

She nodded. "Usually. Except not now. Dinner? Tonight? My place?"

"Sure."

She backed away, half-angry with herself for giving into

this unruly need and half-satisfied, knowing she had no choice. "Good." She turned to leave.

"Rebecca, I think you've forgotten something."

She smiled and turned, walked up to him and kissed him lightly on the lips. "This?"

He kissed her and it wasn't lightly, before pulling away and bringing the basket into her hands. "No, this."

She backed away, embarrassed. "Thank you." She turned just as Gemma entered the studio.

"Becks! I didn't expect to see you here! Didn't you get my text?"

"No. Well, maybe. I was just about here by that time so I thought I'd drop these off."

Gemma glanced at Morgan who was still buttoning up his shirt. She raised her eyebrows. "And see Morgan?"

"Yes, well. Morgan was here. So it would have been rude not to."

"Absolutely. Fancy a coffee?"

"No, I have to get back. Sorry, I can't stay. I have to be at the Information Office. Have some people to show around the Observatory in an hour."

"Sure. Fancy dinner tonight?"

Rebecca glanced at Morgan but he was picking up his hammer. "Not tonight."

"Then how about Friday?"

"Sounds great."

Gemma gave Rebecca a hug and Rebecca walked outside into the bright sunshine with her. "That is, unless you're having your baby by then."

"I hope so. This must be the longest pregnancy known to woman."

"I doubt it. I think you'll find it's pretty much exactly the same."

Gemma laughed. "Trust you to put things into perspective." Rebecca got into the car and Gemma pushed the door closed behind her. "Safe drive home," she called through the open window.

But it wasn't Gemma who Rebecca was thinking of as she drove off back to Shelter Springs across the plains that still held a sheen of frost on them in places. It was her reaction to Morgan. She didn't do things like that. She didn't react like that, never had and had promised herself that she never would. That primitive lust was a new feeling for her. Damn. She was angry with her body for responding but she was more angry about the fact that she couldn't stop herself. She needed to see Morgan as soon as possible. Did that mean she was like her birth father after all?

Morgan went back to work, fully aroused and with a heavy heart.

It was the heavy heart that troubled him the most. That damned text. Why did she keep contacting him, refusing to tell him what he needed to know, only demanding things he couldn't give? Damn the woman. But his anger for the woman who'd betrayed him couldn't wipe out the lust that filled his body.

He could still smell Rebecca's fragrance, could still taste her on his lips. And he knew he'd get no rest until he saw her again. She'd made it clear she wanted him. And he wasn't going to disappoint.

CHAPTER THREE

As Rebecca scanned her bedroom for the nth time, she wondered why on earth she'd invited Morgan to dinner. She hadn't planned it, just as she hadn't planned the kiss. She hadn't really planned—well maybe just a little—to see Morgan in the first place. She'd gone to Glencoe under the pretense that she was going to visit Gemma. Well, that pretense had been shot sky high when she hadn't answered Gemma's text.

Up until now Rebecca hadn't actually realized that she could fool herself quite so successfully. But there it was. The truth for all—well, her and Morgan anyway—to see.

She smoothed the king-size white feather duvet which lay like a cloud on top of the bed. Why on earth was she even doing that? There was no way he was coming in here. She didn't sleep around. She had a list and a plan and she was determined to stick to it.

Despite her best intentions she checked to make sure her clothes were tidily put away. No ornaments or girly things adorned her dressing table. The only things left out on her bedside table were a pile of reference books and an e-reader.

She walked through the sunny yellow hallway, lit only by a single lamp that she'd picked up cheap in a charity shop, which stood on the kauri table she'd bought in New Zealand. She went through to the kitchen and stirred the sauce, peeked into the oven—the chicken was doing nicely—and made sure the vegetables were ready to steam. She moved the platter of antipasto slightly to one side. Then back again.

This was ridiculous! She looked down at her dress. Why on earth was she wearing a dress? She never wore a dress. She'd change.

She re-entered her bedroom, slipped out of her dress and walked to the wardrobe, trying to decide between her jeans and the black trousers she wore for work, when the old-fashioned door chimes rang. She grabbed her bulky dressing gown and pulled it on. She took a deep breath in a vain attempt to quiet her racing heart and went into the hall to open the door.

Morgan stood with a bottle of wine in one hand and a bunch of flowers in the other. He looked so ill at ease that she only just restrained from laughing. Instead she smiled. "Morgan!"

He answered her smile with one of his own which quickly disintegrated into his usual frown.

"You *are* expecting me, aren't you?"

"Yes, of course. Come in."

She opened the door wider and he stepped inside, filling the small place. He was wearing her favorite worn jeans and a battered black leather jacket, undone—did this man never feel the cold?—revealing an open-necked shirt underneath. With an effort she raised her gaze from his chest, up his tanned neck and to his face. A blush bloomed out of nowhere at the sight of those blue eyes accentuated by his tan. She turned away quickly as she tried to hide her reaction.

"This way," she mumbled and led him to the kitchen. She immediately went behind the kitchen bench and busied herself getting a couple of wine glasses from the cupboard, taking surreptitious calming deep breaths as she did so. But when she stood up and found herself face to face with him again, she realized she could take all the deep breaths she liked, but it wouldn't make any difference. Her heart still pounded and the blush still lingered.

He held out the flowers to her. "For you."

"Thank you. You shouldn't have gone to so much trouble. You must have had to get them in from Christchurch." She placed them in a vase, glad of the chance to move away. It felt as if he was pulling her into his orbit like an enormous sun. Sure made her feel as hot. She adjusted the collar of her dressing gown.

"No trouble."

"Would you like a drink?"

"Beer, please."

She took a beer from the fridge and held it out to him. His gaze fixed on her and she felt a flash of desire sweep through her. How did he do that, with just one look? Then he took the beer and his fingers brushed hers. Her stomach tripped and the flash of desire settled low inside her, into a needy ache.

Her gaze roamed hungrily over him before settling on his hair, where his sexy curls were pushed off his face. She felt an overwhelming urge to put her finger into one and pull it straight, to feel the strength of the spring. Just as well it was usually covered up. "You're not wearing your hat."

"I didn't think I'd need it."

"No, of course not. It's just your hair. It's well..." She trailed off, suddenly realizing she was only going to embarrass herself if she continued. You didn't invite a man into your home for the first time and tell him how wonderful his hair was. "I hope you like the beer. I don't usually drink beer so I didn't know what sort to buy."

"I'll like it." He hadn't even looked at it. He slipped off his jacket and hooked it on the back of the bar stool.

"You're wearing a new shirt." The grid-like creases were still evident from the box in which it'd been bought. Her gaze dropped to his jeans. They were still the same, thank goodness. Worn in all the right places.

"Yes. And you're wearing a dressing gown."

She pressed her hand to the soft cloth. She'd been so absorbed in him that she'd almost forgotten what she was wearing. "Yes, I'm sorry, I was changing. I'll go and finish off. Make yourself comfortable."

She went back into the hall and into her bedroom where she picked up the first thing she could find—the dress she'd just taken off and slipped it back on again, tugging up the zip quickly.

She hesitated on the threshold and watched Morgan take a swig of beer from the bottle—he'd left the glass on the bench—and look about the open-plan kitchen-family room. It was small and homey, decorated with bright colors and pre-loved furniture, but it was perfect in her eyes—it was the home she'd wanted all her life. She was used to being either by herself in it, or in the company of Gemma, so it was strange seeing him there. He took up so much more space than she and Gemma had—both physically and in some other way which she couldn't describe.

She walked up slowly behind him and followed his gaze

to the family photo of her and her mother and father standing stiffly outside a school hall.

"That's my family."

"You don't look much alike."

Her smile faded. "No, I'm nothing like either of them —not in coloring, height or shape. There was no way they could hide the fact that I was adopted when I was growing up. They had to tell me pretty much straight away."

"How did you take it?"

"You know? It sounds awful but I was relieved." She picked up the photo. "It was like a mystery solved because we were poles apart. I guess they loved me in their own way but they certainly didn't express it. We were really very different. They didn't understand why I liked to study and I didn't understand why they didn't talk to each other, why they seemed so unhappy. It made me determined to be more careful than they were when it came to choosing who I marry."

"How do you mean?"

"Mum told me they met on a blind date and were married a few months later. They were in their thirties then." She shrugged. "I guess they felt pressure to marry. It wasn't an easy atmosphere to grow up in."

"That's not how I imagined you being brought up."

"You imagined how I was brought up?"

It was Morgan's turn to feel ill-at-ease. He shifted uncomfortably. "Just imagined you'd have had a sweet life, comfortable, with parents who gave you everything you wanted."

"You think I'm spoiled?"

"No! What I'm trying to say is that... that... you're so..." He swept his hands through his hair in a gesture of confusion. "I don't know. It's just that you seem so... kind of... perfect, really."

"Ha!" She grinned. "I don't know what made you think that!" She placed the photo back on the sideboard. "This is as close as we came to perfect. I think my parents were actually proud of me. I'd just passed my Physics Aptitude Test for entrance into the University of Oxford. I was one of the few pupils at my school to take it, let alone pass it. I guess that's why my teacher took the photo."

"You're very clever." He turned away from her suddenly and took a swig of his beer from the bottle.

"Yes," she replied matter-of-factly. "Would you mind opening the wine? I have to baste the potatoes." A blast of hot air flooded the room as she bent down and opened the oven, and spooned the hot juices over the crisp, seasoned roast potatoes.

"It smells good."

His voice was right behind her and she had to focus not to burn herself. "It's the seasoning I've used." She closed the oven door and reached for the wooden spoon to stir the sauce that was bubbling on the stovetop.

"Stop right there." His commanding voice thrilled her to the core and she realized that at that moment she'd have done anything he told her to do.

Her skin prickled as his hand brushed the nape of her neck before taking the thick skein of hair that fell down her back and moving it to one side. She held her breath. Was he going to kiss her? Her heart raced but she stood unmoving, as her complete attention was focused on the movement of his hands on her body. Then she felt the drag of her zip closing.

"You hadn't pulled it right up."

She exhaled, shook her head and her hair shifted back

into place over his hands which hadn't moved. Then she turned and looked up at him, feeling his presence in every fiber of her body, wanting him to kiss her, as he had in the studio.

It was Morgan who broke the silence. "I think something's burning."

His words, together with the smell of burning sauce caused her to turn around and slide the pan off the heat. She swore under her breath. What on earth was happening to her? She never did things like that. She pushed her fingers through her hair and turned around. "Okay, I'm going to leave the kitchen alone for a few moments and have a glass of wine."

She sucked in another breath as he reached toward her, and then beyond her, picked up the wine and unscrewed the top. "Glass?"

"Yes," she exhaled, holding out the glass for him to fill. "I'm not ready to drink wine from the bottle just yet."

After he'd finished pouring she walked determinedly away from him and took a large swig. Relax, she told herself. She could do this. She turned around, giving him what she hoped was an easy smile. But from his brief frown she thought she'd probably failed.

"Come and sit down, dinner won't be long."

He gave a half-nod, raising his eyebrows as if recognizing what she was doing, what they were *both* doing, but agreeing to play the game. He sat down on the small bright blue chintz settee, looking far too large for it, and once more Rebecca had to force herself to quash a desire to sit across his lap, and let her tongue taste his skin.

She took another hasty glug of wine and sat opposite so the safety of a solid wooden coffee table lay between them. "So, what do you usually do on a Saturday night?"

"Nothing much. Have a few beers with my mates at the pub after we've tended the animals. Or work if there's something needs doing. You?"

She nodded. "Much the same. Except the beers. I don't drink much." She took a hasty gulp of wine. "Except now, obviously." She brought up her drink to her eye level and grimaced at it. "But I like to go to the observatory at night if I can."

"I guess you would, being an astronomer."

"Yes, but my main work is theoretical, computer based, analyzing information that comes in at night. Plus the community work at the Information Office."

"Sounds clever."

She shrugged. "Just one type of clever. I can tell you all about the type of conditions necessary for interstellar gas to convert from atomic to molecular but ask me to wire a plug and I'm stuck."

She glanced down at his strong hands and lost her train of thought. She took another swig of wine. When she looked up at him he was looking at her thoughtfully. For a horrible moment she wondered if she'd put him off her by something she'd said. "Is anything wrong?"

"No. But I'm curious. Why did you invite me here, Rebecca? You must have men queueing to spend time with you."

She nearly spilt her wine. "Queueing? I don't think so. You didn't overtake a line of men on the garden path, did you?"

But his face didn't break into the smile she'd hoped for. "You know what I mean. Do you really *not* have a boyfriend?"

She shook her head. "No." She shrugged. "I mean sometimes I've been asked out but more often than not I get bored. They either talk too much—I'm not sure about what because I forget to listen. Or they try to ply me with food and drink to stop me talking about my favorite subjects and get me into bed."

He didn't say anything for a few moments. "Do they succeed?"

"No, I don't sleep around."

He sat back and took a swig of beer and nodded. "So you're not interested in a relationship?"

"Only with someone who fits my criteria."

"Criteria? What do you mean?"

"I have a list of requirements."

That made him laugh. "For real?"

"Yes, of course. I need to make sure that I can share my interests with someone. That we're compatible. What better way than to work it out scientifically?"

"I guess. Although most people leave it to chance."

"And what a mess most people make of it."

"That's true. Yes, maybe you have something there."

"And maybe *you* should make out a list."

"No, no need."

"Because?"

He looked at her with an intensity that drove deep inside her, leaving a hot throbbing desire. "I don't need a list to tell me what I need to know about someone, what I need to know about *anything* I want."

"Oh..." she gulped. "But without thinking it through properly you might"—she shrugged—"you know, make a mistake."

"I have my own system."

"And that is?" she replied faintly.

"I use my senses." His gaze roved around her face. "Say I'm in the market for a new horse. First thing I'd do is check her over with my eyes. If she looks all right then I'll move on in."

"On *in?*"

"Um," he nodded. "Get a bit closer." He dipped his head to hers and she could feel his breath on her neck. "I'd smell her." He drew closer still and then pulled away.

"What does smell tell you?"

"Everything."

"Like?"

"I can't describe it. It's instinctive. It either works... or it doesn't." He leaned back into the settee again and watched her from under a lowered brow. "It'll tell you more than a list can. You should try it some time."

"And then..."

"I'd touch her. Run my hand over her head, neck, and belly, to see how she reacts; to see how she feels. I need her to trust me, not to be too skittish."

"Oh," she exhaled, not realizing she'd been holding her breath. "Yes, skittish isn't good." She leaned in, almost offering her face to his touch.

As she moved closer, her gaze drinking in the masculine frame, the earthy smell of him filled her. Her heart was thudding and the way his eyes lingered on her continued to do strange things deep inside her. "Um," she said trying to gather the remnants of control together. She took another sip of her wine and then noticed it was empty. She put the glass firmly onto the table. She needed to get up, move away from him, go and finish off the dinner. Then she made a mistake, she stood up and didn't move. His eyes held hers in a confident challenge. Slowly he reached up and held out his hand to her. She didn't hesitate, but reached over and touched the tips of his fingers with hers.

She could see her fingers were trembling slightly, but

his weren't. He slid his fingers through hers, and closed his large hand around her small one. He didn't tug her to him, she didn't think he did anyway, but somehow she stepped around the table and over to him as if compelled by some force.

He remained seated as his other hand slid down her bare arm. He turned it over and stroked his finger down the pale underside. "Like silk," he murmured.

There was a moment when she could have pulled back. But she didn't. He gave her that moment but she didn't take it. Instead she gripped his hand as it was about to slip from hers and she pulled herself to him as if grabbing onto a life raft. Before she knew it, she was standing between his legs. She didn't have to lower her head far to place her free hand against his stubbly cheek, holding him or her steady, she wasn't sure which, as she brushed her lips against his.

If she thought it would be a tentative kiss, she hadn't reckoned on his needs. With one swift movement he pulled her onto his lap and had her in his arms, his mouth on hers, his tongue entering her, filling her with a hot sweet neediness deep inside. She moaned as his kiss deepened and she pressed her fingers into his thick golden hair, gripping the curls at the ends and curling them around and around her fingers until she held him as firmly as he held her.

His hands slid along over her shoulders, down into the small of her back and then cupped her bottom, lifting her as she moved her bent knees to either side of his thighs. Her dress rode up her legs and she wriggled closer, her fingernails raking over his scalp as she gripped his head.

She felt his groan travel through her body, disappearing deep into her belly... and further. As she felt his hands thrust up inside her dress, she gasped and pulled away from his kiss.

But it wasn't distance she wanted, it was a more intimate connection. She knelt a little higher and his lips moved to her neck, branding her with hot kisses that began a downward trail until they found the top of her breasts.

She arched back and he slid down the zip of her dress, releasing it at the front, pulling it down until her black bra was revealed. She glanced down at the only sexy bra she owned and was glad she'd managed to fool herself quite so thoroughly into wearing her best underwear.

"You're so beautiful," he murmured. He stroked the soft white mounds of her breasts over her bra, before following his finger with his lips. She gasped as his tongue dipped between her breasts.

"Undo it," she murmured.

He didn't need further prompting, and quickly flicked open her bra.

She felt the vibration of his groan against her tender skin as he pressed his lips to her, trailing hot kisses. She gasped and arched backward. He closed his mouth around her breast and she cried out with shock as the sensations shot through her, turning her weak with need.

He must have sensed her weakness because he moved his hands around her back, holding her steady and firm while he gave his complete attention to first one breast, and then another.

He pulled away. "Look at you," he said huskily. She looked down to see her pale breasts exposed and heaving as she tried to catch her breath.

Suddenly seeing herself like that brought her back to reality with a jolt, and she tried to cover herself. But he put his hand over hers and gave her such a look of tenderness that it stopped her in her tracks. "You're so beautiful." He kissed her briefly before moving his attention back to her breasts.

Pure thick bliss filled her veins, making her languid and needy at the same time. She had no more thought of stopping. She was completely governed by her senses as she writhed against him, her breathing coming in sharp pants.

He pulled away and she began to undo the button on his shirt. She was desperate to see him, to feel him, to kiss his body, as he was kissing and tasting hers.

She pushed aside the soft stuff of his shirt and fanned her fingers over his chest, relishing the sensation of his chest hair against her sensitive fingertips, her palms caressing the muscles which tensed under her touch. She'd never been so turned on by anyone before. What was she thinking? She'd never *done* anything like this before.

She pressed her lips against his chest, kissing, tasting, feeling, breathing him in. She wanted all of him. It was only the touch of his fingers threading through her hair that stopped her. He shifted her hands until they were bracketed her cheeks, drawing her up to face him.

"Rebecca, are you sure?"

She swallowed, trying to rouse herself from the desire that pounded through her blood. She nodded. "Sure, I'm sure." She brushed her lips against his but he didn't respond. She pulled back, suddenly alarmed. "Are you?"

He closed his eyes briefly and when he opened them again she could see the dark-filled lust which gave her her answer. He pulled her head to his and kissed her with an urgency which told her all she needed to know.

His mouth explored hers with a sensitivity that surprised her. The strength was there in his hands around her head, and he wasn't using it to force her into anything, simply to hold her while his tongue explored her mouth and tongue with a restraint that she didn't share. His every touch, every sweep of his tongue against hers ratcheted up the tension, making her more and more impatient. Her hands trembled with need as they moved over his body.

She moaned as his hands once again swept under her dress. She pulled away from him, panting. "Come on." She clambered off him and tried to tug him to standing. But she realized she wasn't anywhere near strong enough to force him to do anything he didn't want to do.

But he rose anyway and lifted her into his arms. Her legs curled around his hips as their mouths met again. This time she could feel his restraint beginning to crack as he moved more urgently against her, gripping her hips firmly to his. It was driving her crazy. She pulled away. "The bedroom," she managed to whisper croakily, hardly recognizing her husky sex-filled voice.

He didn't need telling twice and he carried her along the hallway. She kicked the door open with her foot and he walked through and they fell onto her feather-soft duvet. His hands moved quickly and by the time he stood up, she was already half-undressed. She knelt on the edge of the bed and fumbled with his zip.

With his clothes off, she rolled back on her heels and swallowed, her whole body trembling. She'd only been to bed with a few men, mainly to see what the fuss was about, looking upon it as a scientific experiment more than anything else. Never before had she felt so filled with lust as now.

And then she looked up into his eyes and there was no more time for reflection, only action. She fell back onto the bed and he climbed on after her and gave her exactly what she'd been needing, what she'd been dreaming of, ever since their first kiss.

. . .

Rebecca awoke in his arms and didn't move for a few minutes as she let what had happened sink into her. She was cradled in his strong arms, her head resting on his biceps, their legs tangled. Her body was spent—a delicious blending of aching and satiation. But overwhelming everything was a feeling of fear. Because the woman she'd become when she'd made love had disappeared and she was Rebecca the scientist once more. And she'd just had sex with a man who was almost a stranger. What kind of woman was she?

She blushed as she remembered how she'd acted, the things she'd done. She was sex mad. What had her adoptive father always said? The apple doesn't fall far from the tree. She wriggled out from under Morgan's sleeping arms. He merely rolled onto his back and fell back into a deep sleep once more. She pulled up her knees to her chin and looked down at him. She wanted to cry.

She'd entered into her brief previous sexual relationships with the control of an experiment and had convinced herself that she was nothing like her birth father. Yes, it'd felt satisfactory, but she'd always had control. But this? This was sexual madness!

Hot tears pressed behind her lids and she rose and pulled on her dressing gown, quietly walking to the bathroom to shower. She didn't know how long she stood there, under the stream of hot water. She didn't soap herself, didn't move. Just cried. Cried for the scientist she'd thought she was, who had proved illusory, cried for the woman who'd been revealed. Not like her adoptive parents, not like her birth mother, but a woman with the uncontrollable sexuality of her birth father—a man who'd raped and planted his seed in her birth mother.

She rested her forehead against the steamy shower,

rocking it as she shook her head in denial. Just because she enjoyed sex it didn't make her bad—not bad like her birth father—did it? No, it didn't. She knew it didn't. But why did the tears continue to flow? Why did she feel as though Morgan had unleashed a monster, a monster that scared the hell out of her?

CHAPTER FOUR

M organ turned his back on the people milling around Glencoe, whistled for Annie and cantered off toward the high country. Snow was forecast and the stragglers needed to be brought in. As Callum had given him the manager's role while he tried to recruit someone, Morgan could have delegated the responsibility. But not today. Today he needed the open air, to work with the sheep and time to think.

It'd had been two weeks since that night with Rebecca. Two weeks, fourteen days and who knew how many hours? Rebecca would, of course. She had the mind of a computer and had been terrified when it had lapsed and the needs of her body had taken over and she'd found herself in bed with him.

He'd been over and over it. He'd not forced himself on her. She'd made it plain she'd wanted him. What else could he have done? Refused her? That would be contrary to the instincts of any red-blooded man. No, he'd just been himself and that obviously wasn't what she'd wanted. Maybe at the time. But not after. Not when she'd had time to think it through.

Seems she'd come to realize what he already knew—he didn't deserve someone like her. He was her inferior in every way. Pity she hadn't realized that before they'd had sex.

Before then he'd been able to enjoy seeing her, appreciate her beauty and her appealing character—so different from the other women who'd come his way. But now it had gone further than that and he couldn't get her out of his mind. He was obsessed with her, he craved her like a drug. He relived every moment he'd spent with her over and over again. No matter how he tried to contain it, his need for her only increased.

Even now his mind was filled with the image of her, sitting astride him, her head thrust back—her eyes closed and mouth a perfect O—as the tension in her body released. But the worst image, the one that taunted him and haunted him was of her telling him to leave. No explanation. No politeness, no... anything. Just a clear instruction as if he'd done what he'd come to do and now it was time for him to clear out. She'd got what she wanted and he could be sent packing, like the hired hand he was.

And he'd left, just as she'd wanted. Quietly. And he wouldn't bother her again. That's why he was heading for the hills while Callum and Gemma's family and friends—including Rebecca—arrived at Glencoe after christening baby Violet at church. He could hear them arriving now, the stream of cars winding up the road to Glencoe from Shelter Springs.

Callum had invited him to attend but Morgan knew his place and had declined. Despite his parents, Callum was a good man—one Morgan liked and respected. But there was no way he'd attend Callum's kid's christening. It wasn't his world. And he didn't want to risk running into Rebecca only to be rebuffed once more. So he'd made his excuses and he'd been off at sunrise and wouldn't be back until the last of them had left.

He glanced back at Glencoe, people issuing forth from the cars, milling around the grand old house in the cold sunshine. Inside he knew the fires would be roaring and the champagne flowing. But not for him.

He urged his horse forward. He'd done what he'd come to do, seen the place his mother had talked about incessantly as he'd grown up. Now it was time to leave. He'd give it another six months and then, by the beginning of summer, he'd be out of here. Back to wandering, back to staying only a season at a time in a place before moving on. No roots: that's the way he liked it. He should never have come here in the first place.

"Gemma," called Rebecca. "I'd like you to meet Martin."

Gemma tore herself away from Callum, Dallas Mackenzie—the eldest brother— and his wife, Cassandra, who was holding their younger daughter, Daniella, and extended her hand to Martin. "Martin! Good to meet you at last." She cast a quick cheeky look at Rebecca. "Rebecca has told me so much about you."

Martin turned away from looking at Callum and raised his eyebrows. "Really?"

Rebecca shot Gemma a narrowed glance. "I was telling Gemma about the GAMA survey we're working on."

"And you were interested?" he asked Gemma.

Gemma looked uncomfortable and shrugged noncommittally.

Martin grinned. "Thought not. But you might find my other project more interesting. I'm working with a historian on the history of the observatory. One of the astronomers has to be involved and my first degree was in history."

"Have you talked to Callum? He'd be interested. The land the observatory's on was originally Glencoe land, I believe."

"I'd *love* to talk to him." He looked across at Callum and his gaze lingered there. "He's very tall, isn't he?"

Gemma and Rebecca exchanged puzzled glances.

"Oh well, sure. I'll introduce you." Gemma shrugged at Rebecca behind Martin's back and followed him over to Callum.

Rebecca wandered over to the French windows outside which children played in the winter sunshine and looked out to the snow-capped mountains. She'd thought she might have seen Morgan here. It had only been when Callum had mentioned that Morgan wasn't coming, that he was going out to fetch some stray merino, that Rebecca had decided to bring her friend, Martin. She had to get herself back on track. After all, Martin fit all her criteria. She couldn't risk being with Morgan again. Her evening with him had been a disastrous mistake. It'd had shown her what her true nature was like and it had scared her to death.

She glanced at Martin who was now talking animatedly to Callum who appeared to be totally ignoring him. He only had eyes for Violet, his baby girl who was sleeping peacefully in his arms. Martin was handsome. She knew that intellectually. Then why didn't the same strange sensations overtake her body as they did when she was with Morgan?

She folded her arms defensively and took a quick sip of orange juice. She hadn't drunk any alcohol since that night with Morgan. Not that she could blame a few glasses of wine on what happened. If only she could.

No, it was just as well Martin didn't produce the same sensations in her. She didn't want to lose control again. It made her believe that genetically she was more like her depraved birth father than she'd ever allowed herself to consider. And the thought sickened her. She'd rather have a celibate marriage than descend to the level of an animal where she was driven purely by instinct. Who knew where that would take her? But she *did* know. That complete abandon when he... She closed her eyes and turned her back to the party as the memory of how Morgan had held her in his arms overtook her, sending shivers of melting heat through her body. Her thumb absently rose from her crossed forearm and flicked over her blouse, grazing her breast.

A hot blush rose within her and she pulled her sensible cardigan tighter around her and cast a furtive glance around. No one had seen. Of course they hadn't. What was there to see? It was all in her head.

Martin was now standing on his own, but he wasn't looking across at her. He was looking at Callum's younger brother James, who'd just entered the room. James caught her eye and came over.

"Rebecca!" He kissed her suavely on both cheeks. "You're looking flushed. Surely not hot on this freezing day?"

"Well," said Rebecca, blushing furiously. Trust James to notice. "It *is* quite warm in here."

He shrugged. "Whatever, you look as beautiful as always."

Rebecca racked her brains, trying to think of something to divert James. "Gemma tells me you're into wine making."

"Yes, I own a winery in Napa Valley as well as other holdings in Australia. I'm always on the lookout for new opportunities." He grinned and she felt the full force of his charm once more. "It's always good to keep your eyes open." He inclined his head to hers. "I wouldn't want to miss anything."

She pulled away with a narrowed glance. "I doubt you miss much." Funny, James had most of the qualities she wanted—though he obviously wasn't ready to make any commitments—but there wasn't a real spark of attraction there, either.

"True." He glanced over at Martin. "Including your friend over there. You do know he's—"

"James!" Cassandra, Dallas's wife and James's brother-in-law, greeted James. "How are you?"

Cassandra always made Rebecca feel a little uncomfortable. She was so beautiful, so talented and so sophisticated that Rebecca murmured her excuses and slipped away.

She looked briefly over at Martin, not particularly wanting to join him but feeling a certain duty. After all he was here with her. But she could see he was enjoying himself, talking with a group of farm hands out on the veranda. She briefly wondered what on earth they could be talking about that he was finding so enjoyable. And then wondered what James had been about to say. She dismissed both ideas. For some reason she wasn't in the mood to contemplate her wish list, or her future. Instead she wandered back to the French Windows and looked out. She glanced around her and stepped outside. The gardens were empty now that the short daylight of winter was waning.

She pulled her cardigan around her and shivered but continued along the old veranda around to where she could see the outline of the mountains, the red of the sunset still caught in their snow-capped tops. It was stunning but something was missing. She wished Morgan was here. But he wasn't and there wasn't any point in standing outside, shivering in the cold, she told herself sternly.

She turned quickly to enter the front door and slapped straight into Morgan—his shirt ripped and grimy. She made a strangled sound of surprise and would have been knocked off balance if it hadn't been for Morgan, instinctively reaching for her and gripping her arms. She could feel herself respond, like it or not. She almost melted against him and for one brief moment their heads came together, their mouths so close it wouldn't have taken much for them to touch, for them to kiss, for them to explore each other, just as they'd done only a few short weeks ago.

If Rebecca had been hoping she'd forget how he'd made her feel, she was sorely disappointed. There was nothing she'd forgotten. It all came flooding back.

"Morgan," she breathed, aware her voice had lowered huskily. She cleared her throat, annoyed. "Are you okay?"

"What?" For a brief moment he looked confused.

She had to get a grip on herself. She looked down at his hand, wrapped in a piece of his shirt, stained with blood. "What have you done to your hand?"

His hands dropped to his sides and he pulled back. "It's nothing. Had a bit of trouble getting some sheep out of a gully."

Just at that moment Callum came around the corner. He lifted his brows with his characteristic understatement.

"I found them," said Morgan.

Callum glanced down at Morgan's hand. "And it looks like they found your hand."

"Yeah. One of the stragglers was a bit hard to handle and slammed my hand against a rock. It's fine. Nothing broken." Morgan turned away and narrowed his eyes as if focusing on the distant hills.

For the first time, Rebecca was struck not just by Callum and Morgan's physical similarity but by their personalities. Both preferred brevity in conversation and both were down-to-earth people who totally understood each other.

"Better get it cleaned up," said Callum.

"I'll do it," said Rebecca, picking up Morgan's hand and gingerly unwrapping the makeshift bandage.

"There's a First Aid kit in the downstairs bathroom," said Callum. "I'll go and let Gemma know. She may have something else you can use."

Callum went back inside and Rebecca pulled Morgan toward the door but he resisted.

He shrugged. "I can't go inside looking like this."

"Why on earth not?"

"Lady Mackenzie won't like it."

"She'll have to lump it."

She turned back and took him by the wrist and pulled him inside. Immediately conversation stalled and all eyes turned to them. Rebecca was grateful when Martin made a beeline for them. "We've not met," he said extending his hand to Morgan who looked at it and then turned away.

The awkward moment was interrupted by Gemma who burst through the people who'd gathered to stare. "Are you okay?"

"I'm fine. Just a scratch."

"It's *not* a scratch. Look at his hand, Gemma." Rebecca grabbed the bloodied bandaged hand and held it up for all to see. There was a collective gasp from around the room.

"Come on, I'll take you the bathroom. We can clean it up there."

Morgan followed Gemma, and Rebecca brought up the rear, watching the reaction of the other invited guests with interest. Particularly Lady Mackenzie whose look of severe distaste would have been sufficient to make Rebecca hate her. But then she spoke.

"What is *he* doing here? I thought Callum had arranged a barbecue for the hired hands."

"Looks like the barbecue got out of hand," snickered one of the guests. "Some kind of fight probably."

"Really. Grown men should know better than to fight. That's no way to behave in civilized company."

That was too much for Rebecca and she went up to Lady Mackenzie. "Morgan wasn't fighting. He was risking his life bringing in some sheep stuck in a gully, while you've all"—she shot a deadly look at the people Lady Mackenzie had gathered around her—"been here drinking champagne." Rebecca suddenly wanted to say a whole lot more. Lady Mackenzie had given Gemma a really hard time over the past year and Gemma had bitten her tongue time and time again. But, Rebecca didn't want to make things more difficult for Gemma than they already were, so she turned away to follow an astounded looking Morgan and Gemma who'd paused by the door.

"She's a friend of Gemma's," Lady Mackenzie said by way of explanation to the group of establishment figures she surrounded herself with. "A little odd." Outraged, Rebecca stopped and slowly turned, her anger filling her.

"Rebecca," said Morgan softly, reaching out to her with his damaged hand.

She looked up immediately and took his hand and the anger passed. She exhaled roughly, all other thoughts dismissed under the power of her connection with this man.

At that moment, James walked by, flashed a brief grin at

Rebecca and walked up to Lady Mackenzie and took her by the arm. "Mother, I have someone I'd like to introduce you to. Lord Caernarvon from Wales is here looking at our merinos."

"Wales, you say." Lady Mackenzie's mood changed in an instant as her handsome youngest, and favorite son worked his charm on her. "Such a strange little country."

"Maybe," he whispered, "but I'm sure you'll like him. He's related to the royal family."

"Really?" Lady Mackenzie was clearly impressed.

Gemma grinned at Rebecca who shook her head and all three of them walked down the hallway.

"Go, Rebecca! That was quite a scene!" Gemma grinned.

"I'm sorry. I shouldn't have said anything. But... the way she's treated you these past months, Gemma, and then that comment about"—she glanced up at Morgan who hadn't taken his eyes from her—"you," she said more softly.

"Oh, I don't mind. I was cheering you on. She's a total witch. Luckily she's not often here. She's usually in Christchurch or annoying Cassandra in Wellington."

Once in the palatial bathroom, Gemma opened the First Aid kit while Rebecca inspected his hand. "At least the bleeding seems to have stopped now."

"Here"—Rebecca glanced warmly to Morgan—"I'll wash your hand."

Gemma rummaged through the kit and selected some ointment. "This should do it." She walked over to Morgan and Gemma, who was trying to wash Morgan's hand under a stream of cold water.

"I can wash my own hands!"

Gemma grinned. "Yeah, but why would you want to, when Rebecca seems to want to do it for you?"

"Good point," Morgan murmured.

Rebecca ignored them both and gently twisted his hand under the running water, angling it to flush away the dirt. "It's not too deep." She took some mild soap from Gemma and cleaned it thoroughly. After she was sure the wound was clean, she wrapped his hand in a towel and patted it dry.

"I can do that," he said pulling the towel toward him.

She tugged it back and continued to dry the wound before carefully wrapping it in gauze.

Gemma looked from one to the other of them. "I'll leave you guys to it. If you want anything you know where I'll be. With my baby, avoiding my scary mother-in-law."

It was just as well Gemma wasn't expecting a reply because Morgan and Rebecca only had eyes for each other.

Rebecca waited until the bathroom door clicked shut.

"Morgan, I'm so sorry."

He flexed his hands. "It wasn't your fault I hurt my hand."

"No!" She suddenly felt embarrassed and looked down as she unwrapped a bandage. "About the other night," she mumbled.

She wrapped the bandage inexpertly around his hand and tied a rough knot, waiting for him to speak. But, instead, his injured fingers curled and moved against hers in a sweeping caress. She looked up abruptly.

"It's okay. You regret it. Stuff like that happens sometimes."

"No! Not to me it doesn't. I've never slept with someone—"

She stopped abruptly.

"Someone like me," he added quietly. "I know I'm not in your league, Rebecca."

"I wasn't going to say that. And I don't know what you're talking about. I don't have a *league*," she emphasized the word, remembering the snobbishness of Lady Mackenzie. "I was going to say, I've never slept with someone who's made me feel so much, who made me forget myself. Morgan West, you scared the life out of me!"

"Scared you? Why? I wouldn't hurt you."

"I know that. And it's not that."

"Then tell me what it is. Tell me and I'll deal with it."

She smiled, admiring Morgan's confidence that he could demolish any obstacle in his path by sheer strength alone. "You can't. I'm frightened of the woman I am when I'm with you. It's that simple."

"You're frightened of losing control."

Her eyes widened with surprise. Morgan had an uncanny way of getting straight to the heart of things.

"Well, yes."

"You *can* trust me, you know. If you lose control. I'm not going to take more than you want to give. I'm not going to broadcast what we do together. I'm not going to hurt you by throwing that lack of control in your face."

Rebecca opened her mouth to speak. But the tables had turned. It was Morgan who was talking and it was she who was speechless.

His bandaged hand swept up around her waist and he pulled her against him. He kissed the top of her head. "I thought you hated me, Rebecca. I thought you were ashamed you'd made love with someone like me."

She pressed her cheek against his chest. "I don't know why you keep saying things like that. You're you. You're not a class of people. You're simply you. And that's more than enough for anybody."

He exhaled roughly against her head. "You're unique. You're one of a kind."

She smiled and looked up at him. But he wasn't smiling. "I've heard that one before. But I'm not sure it's ever been meant in a nice way."

"*I* mean it in a nice way." And she could see by the serious expression and sudden tenderness in his eyes, that he did. And then he dipped his head and kissed her gently. Immediately the surge of need swept through her and she knew, just knew, that any more and he could have had her there and then on the bathroom floor, where anybody could have walked in, and she wouldn't have cared less.

She pulled, away, breathless, backing away. "No! I can't do this, Morgan. I told you. I'm scared."

"And I told you, you can trust me."

"It's not about trusting you! Don't you understand? It's about trusting *me*."

"No, I don't understand. Help me to."

She walked away, turned to the mirror and swept her fingers under her eyes, determined to blot out the emerging tears that had smudged her mascara. Her face was flushed, her eyes bright and her breathing was ragged. She shook her head and looked up at his reflection in the mirror.

"I'm sorry. I can't. It's humiliating. I don't want to think about it. I don't want to talk about it."

"So, let me get this right. You don't object to me. What stops you from getting close to me is how you feel about your own passion."

She nodded, pursing her lips, scared of what she might say.

He shrugged. "I..." He hesitated as if choosing his word carefully. "*Care* for you, Rebecca."

"And I care for you, Morgan. I don't want to *not* see you. These last few weeks have been, well..."

"Difficult?" he offered.

She nodded mutely.

"Then how about we see each other, get to know each other, without touching, without kissing, without *fear*." He paused. "I don't want to see you afraid. I don't *ever* want to see you afraid. Especially if I'm the cause of it."

"It's not you, not really. It's me. It's difficult, I don't want—"

He pressed his finger lightly against her lips. "I don't want to know if you don't want to tell me. We have time to get to know each other's secrets."

Carefully he withdrew his hand and stepped away, tightening his bandage and putting a tube of salve into his pocket. She waited for him to speak. He pushed his bandaged hand through his wind-blown hair. "I'm a mess."

"No. You look..." she hesitated, before she could say "gorgeous". Telling him he was "gorgeous" wouldn't get her anywhere. "You look fine. Really." She sighed, releasing the tension. "Well, you will after you have a shower."

He nodded. "You like horses, yes?"

"Yes, love them."

"Then I'll show you around the estate. Next weekend. I'll take you riding."

"I'd like that." That must have been the understatement of the year. "Very much," she couldn't help adding, particularly when his eyes crinkled into that warm smile that was somehow contained only in his eyes. "And then on your next day off, I'll show you my world. Show you the stars."

"And I'd like that."

CHAPTER FIVE

"I thought you said you loved horses!" Morgan cupped his hands once more for Rebecca to put her foot in so she could mount the small gray mare he'd chosen for her.

"I do." She put her boot-clad foot into his hands and fell hard against the mare's flank, with a soft oophing noise as she winded herself. "But," she gasped, "I didn't say I knew anything about them."

Throwing discretion to the wind, Morgan placed his other hand under her bottom and pushed her up. Just the feel of her bottom under his hands made him want her. Instinctively he swept his thumb around her curves, sweeping her inner thigh. He pulled back abruptly. What the hell was he doing? He stepped away. Playing with fire, was what he was doing. Thank goodness she hadn't noticed. She was too busy trying to figure out how to move from her current position where she was lying across the horse. "Swing your other leg around."

Suddenly she was there, sitting on top of the mare, looking very proud of herself. "There, see, I knew I could do it."

"Do what? Get on a horse? What about ride one?"

"Well, I haven't done *that* before. But how hard can it be?"

He had to smile, despite his frustration at having to change his plan of where he was going to take her. It was just Rebecca being Rebecca. He was no good at analyzing people, but Rebecca was easy to work out. He knew, instinctively, that she'd never see an obstacle until she'd run into it, fallen over it or jumped clear over it. He wondered which she'd do this time.

"Well, she's a gentle mare. She'll look after you. We'll see how you go."

He jumped up onto his horse and looked over at her. There was a faint look of alarm in her eyes. "You'll be okay. Hold the reins like this, and grip with your thighs. Not your heels," he added as Rebecca's horse started to trot out of the yard. Rebecca bounced on the mare's back and Morgan shook his head and followed her.

"You okay?" He nudged up his hat and glanced at her.

She bounced stoically, gripping onto the saddle and the reins for dear life. She opened her mouth to speak but thought better of it.

"Go a bit faster and then you can sink into a canter. It's easier."

"Faster?" She managed to squeak. "No way."

"Trust me, you'll find it more comfortable. Just gently squeeze your heels into her flanks."

She shook her head determinedly.

"Okay, bring her back to a walk. Pull on your reins a little and she'll ease back. Not too much. She has a soft mouth."

The mare immediately returned to walking pace. Morgan glanced at Rebecca but she made no comment. He had to admire her for that. She'd try her hand at anything and wasn't about to moan and whinge if it proved difficult. She was a brave wee thing.

"So, where are we headed?" She even managed a brief worried smile.

He pointed to the foothills. "Thought I'd show you the view from the ridge."

"Oh, that's quite a long way really isn't it?" She glanced uneasily down at her horse.

"That depends."

"On?"

"On whether you get your mare going above a walk."

"For the moment, she's fine. We're just getting used to each other."

He grunted. Putting off the evil moment when she'd have to learn how to hang on to a horse in motion, more like. Still, it was up to her. "Okay."

Despite the brisk wind, the sun was bright and warm for midwinter. At least Rebecca was dressed for the conditions in her thick coat, boots and hat, even if she hadn't the first idea how to ride. Although she was beginning to look more comfortable with each step.

Morgan sank into the easy silence that was his usual response to the massive emptiness of the Mackenzie basin. He squinted into the distance under the bright golden light and marveled again at how at home he felt here.

"You look like you belong here."

Startled, Morgan turned to Rebecca. He could read her like a book. Seemed like she could do the same with him. He just hoped she couldn't read *all* his thoughts. "What?"

"Belong. You look like you're a part of this place. How long have you been here?"

"Nearly a year and a half. When did you arrive?"

"Two years ago. And I knew immediately this place was home. What more could a girl want? A small town where everyone knows everyone else, friends and of course, stars."

"There are stars everywhere."

"Not like here. We're so far from the big cities, the sky is darker, there's minimal light pollution, and combined with the powerful telescopes up at the observatory, it's a first-class sky."

"A first-class sky." He glanced upward. "I guess it is."

"So if you're not from around here, what made you come?"

He groaned inwardly. It didn't look like he'd evaded the questioning. "I move around. Worked on most of the big stations in Canterbury and Otago."

"And so you just came here. Because..."

"Because I heard there was a job going and I'd heard about this place before." He knew he'd said too much even before she replied.

"Ah-ha! So you'd heard about Glencoe before. How come? What had you heard? Tell all!"

He was silent for a little while, wondering how to reply. His past was his alone and he never talked to people about it. If you told someone something, they had power over you. But Rebecca was different. He cleared his throat. "My mother was from around here."

Rebecca was evidently so surprised that she pulled her horse to a standstill. He walked on a few paces and then turned in his saddle. "It'll take us even longer to get to the ridge if your horse doesn't move."

"Oh! Sure." She looked uncertainly at her horse.

"Just flick the reins. She'll go."

Rebecca did, and the mare went. "Your mother was from here, you say?"

"Um." Morgan regretted having told her already. "Looks like it'll be an easy ride over to the ridge. Ready to go a bit faster yet?"

"No." She had her clear gaze fixed on him in such a determined way that he realized he wasn't going to get out of it by simply changing the subject. "So where was your mother from? Shelter Springs?"

"Thereabouts."

"*Where*abouts exactly?"

Morgan tilted up his hat and looked around the ring of snow-capped mountains as if for inspiration. But there was none. He sighed, lifted his hat, thrust his fingers through his hair and pushed his hat back into place. "Glencoe," he murmured. Maybe the truth would stop her.

Rebecca inadvertently urged her mare into a trot and came bouncing up beside him. For once, her fear was forgotten. "Glencoe?"

He turned to her. "Look, I shouldn't have said anything. No one knows. Not Callum, nor anyone else. And I want it kept that way."

"Why? Is it a secret?"

"It's *not* a secret!" he said, too forcibly. "Not *exactly*," he said, quieter. "Look, I'm a private man. I like my personal life to be just that. It's how I like it."

She nodded. She might understand but he could tell by the obstinate jut of her jaw that she wasn't going to let it go.

"Okay. I won't say anything."

He narrowed his gaze, suspicious. "Good."

"Provided you tell me *everything*," she said with a disarming smile. He pulled up his horse so sharply that Rebecca yelped in surprise.

"Are you blackmailing me?"

He should have been annoyed but the naughty sweetness of her smile did other things to him instead. He shifted in his saddle and was glad of the heavy coat that came to his thighs.

"Yes, I am."

"Then I have no choice."

She tilted that cheeky face making her even more adorable. "No, you don't."

She'd thought she'd won. He'd have to show her she hadn't. He came closer to her and lowered his head to hers and spoke confidentially. "Now, what I want you to remember is..." His fingers took hers from her reins and guided them gently to the pommel on the saddle. Then he smoothed his hands down the flank of the horse as her eyes remained on his.

"Yes," she said breathlessly. The wind seemed to die down around them and there was only the sun, the fresh air, the warmth of the horses, and their faces, close to each other.

He gently rubbed the horse's flank and then raised his hand. "Is... to grip with your thighs and hold onto the saddle." She still hadn't got it, he could tell by her frown. He drew away and lightly smacked Rebecca's horse on the rump. Rebecca yelped again as the horse moved smoothly away, gathering speed gently, allowing Rebecca time to tighten her grip.

Morgan followed close behind. For a brief moment, as he watched Rebecca bounce almost uncontrollably on the horse's back, he wondered if he'd gone too far. But he knew the mare was sensitive and was taking it easy on Rebecca. He trusted the horse and he was proven right as the mare fell into a rolling canter. Rebecca adjusted to the speed and followed his directions.

He cantered up beside Rebecca. She didn't turn to him.

The reins were flying free and she was holding on to the saddle for dear life, but he could see the flush and smile on her face—it had quickly replaced the initial fear.

"Bastard!" she shouted.

"You're not the first to call me that," he replied with a smile. "You okay?"

She chanced a quick look at him, and he could see she was. A big smile covered her face and her eyes were bright with fun. "You were right. Cantering is easier."

"And it means we'll reach our destination today."

She laughed. And he did too, not only because, with her hat lost and her hair flowing out behind her, she was absolutely beautiful, but also because he'd avoided a difficult conversation.

By the time their horses had picked their way carefully up the narrow ridge to a sheltered plateau overlooking the valley, the sun was high and Rebecca was very hungry.

Morgan jumped off his horse and tethered it loosely to a bush. Her horse walked up to him of her own accord. Morgan turned and took the halter and rubbed the mare's nose. The mare snorted and softly nickered, and moved her head against Morgan's hand, as if returning the affection.

"Good girl," Morgan murmured, patting her neck. Rebecca's heart swelled. He might be awkward with people, but Morgan West had a heart of pure gold.

"Am I?" She grinned at him.

"No, *you're* a bad girl. Pretending you could ride when you hadn't the first idea."

"A girl has to start somewhere. I think I got the hang of it pretty quick."

"Yep. You didn't do too badly." Their gazes clashed and

tangled and held for a few long moments. "Are you going to stay up there forever?"

She laughed, relieved the intense moment had been broken. "Well, I've been trying to get my body to make a move but it seems I've lost all feeling in my legs. I'm not sure I *can* move."

He came around the mare's flank and lifted her off the mare with as much ease as if he were picking up a child. He brought her to the ground but didn't let her go immediately. His fingers fanned out around her sides and pressed into her coat, briefly caressing her skin beneath her layers before releasing his grip. He stepped away.

"So, let's see you move."

For a brief moment she'd forgotten the ache in her legs and higher. She winced as she took a step forward on legs like jelly. He took a blanket out of his pack and threw it on the ground. "Don't have any cushions, I'm afraid, Princess."

She shot him a dark look. "I'm no Princess," she said as she gingerly lowered herself to the ground. She stretched out her legs in front of her. "But I had no idea how hard riding would be on your body."

"You get used to it pretty quick."

She looked out to Glencoe in the distance. "Not quick enough to make the return journey easy."

"We'll sort something out."

"Like Callum's helicopter maybe?"

His eyes narrowed. "If you want helicopters and all that kind of thing you shouldn't have come riding with me."

"You think I want things like that?"

"Sounds like it."

She poked him in the side and he glanced at her. She couldn't help teasing him, he looked so uptight. "Maybe you're right. Maybe I should have accepted James's offer of a champagne picnic in the mountains."

The uptight look vanished under a dark cloud of anger. "He asked you out?"

"Uh-huh."

He jumped up and paced away, hands on hips as he looked out into the blinding sun. She sighed and took pity on him and walked gingerly over to him. "Hey, cowboy, are you going to get in a huff with me because someone asked me out?"

"Of course not. You can go out with whoever you like."

"That's right."

He turned around, his frown lowered over features that were more hurt now, than angry. "I'm surprised James asked you out. He knew—" His eyes searched her face before he turned away abruptly.

"What did he know?"

"Nothing. It doesn't matter. Now do you want to share the contents of your backpack?"

"No, Morgan. No, I don't. Not until you tell me what James knew, which I apparently don't."

"Come on, Rebecca. Do I really have to spell it out? James knows that I"—he sucked in a difficult breath—"that I like you."

"*Like* me," Rebecca repeated. "Um." It was her turn to feel miffed, underwhelmed at his choice of word. "Well, I'm glad you *like* me." She took off her backpack, unbuckled it, and tossed him a package. "I hope you *like* your meat pie too."

He unwrapped it and took a mouthful. He nodded slowly and swallowed. "Like?" He shook his head. "No, I *love* the meat pie." For a moment she wondered if he meant it. Meant that she came further down the love-like scale than a meat pie, but then one of his rare smiles broke out from nowhere and she grunted and threw an apple at him which annoyingly, he caught. "And I love a woman who showers me with food."

"I'm glad I now know how to make myself attractive to you." She bit her lip as soon as she'd said it.

"Believe me, Rebecca, you don't have to do a thing." And when she looked up into his now serious eyes, she knew he was telling the truth.

She smiled back and then pushed herself awkwardly up to standing, not liking the way her thoughts were going. She'd come here to get to know him, not to jump on him. She perched herself on a lichened rock and looked down, over billowing tussock to a lake, the bright turquoise of a glacier, around which mountain beech trees grew.

"You can see forever up here. The mountains, even Aoraki Mt Cook looks so close. It just... I don't know, it just touches you doesn't it? Everything's done on such a grand scale in the Mackenzie Country. I loved it as soon as I saw it and now I can't imagine ever living anywhere else. And imagine living out here. There'd be no lights to interfere with my view of the stars. It'd be perfect."

He leaned back on his elbows, watching her as much as the view. He didn't reply and she began to regret what she'd said. It wasn't like her to be all touchy-feely about things.

She shrugged. "I'm being fanciful. It's just scenery, after all. And you can't live in the middle of nowhere."

He sat up. "It's more than just scenery. You either fit into a place, or you don't. I fit here. And I knew it from the first day I arrived."

"So you're going to stay?"

"I didn't say that. It's my place"—he shrugged—"maybe

simply because it's where my mother came from. But I won't be staying."

"But why on earth not, when you feel so at home here?"

He paused. "It's complicated. I don't like complicated. I don't *do* complicated. So I move on. Makes life easier."

"And more unsatisfactory, I should think," replied Rebecca suddenly feeling irritated by his easy acceptance of a life away from a place that felt like home. Away from a place where she intended to live for as long as she could. Away from her.

"It's unsatisfactory to want more than you can have."

"And what is it you want?"

"Jobwise? I want to get up to work another day. I want to keep on moving."

"But surely you want more than that?"

It was like a shadow passed over his face. She looked up into the sky but it was a brilliant cloudless blue. She looked back at him but the shadow had gone. Perhaps she'd imagined it. He didn't answer, just shook his head.

"But what are your goals?" she continued.

Morgan frowned. "Goals?"

"Yeah, you know those things that everyone has which they're working toward."

A flicker of humor crossed his face. "Oh those. I can imagine you have a few lists with those on."

Rebecca was surprised. "I do, actually."

"Yeah, sure you do. If you have that 'husband list' you told me about, you'll have others. Let me think. One of them will be to do whatever high-falutin' thing you're doing at the observatory. Maybe have a star named after you?"

She grunted. He'd come dangerously close to the truth. "Even if I'd imagined such a thing"—and she had, in Technicolor detail— "it could never happen. It would be named in accordance with the naming convention of the International Astronomical Union."

He lay on his back and looked up at the bright blue, starless sky. "I can just imagine it—the Rebecca star, or maybe the Princess star—it would be very bright and cast all the others into shade."

"Not going to happen. Generally speaking stars don't have proper names."

He rolled on his side and she looked away, not wanting to see that raw intensity in his eyes. "They'll make an exception for you."

"Well..." She peered into the distance, willing the heat that his gaze stirred, to disappear. It didn't. "So that's me sorted. What about you? I don't believe you have any goals."

It worked. He rolled back and looked up at the sky. "No goals. Goals are for sports, for school children. All I want is what I do."

"I don't believe you. There must be something more. That's too... too *content*."

"And *content* bothers you?"

"It doesn't *bother* me. It's just weird. I've never met anyone like you before. There must be something more."

"Uh, uh." He shook his head and plucked a piece of grass and sucked it.

She knelt awkwardly, wincing at the ever-growing ache of discomfort between her legs from the horse ride. "Okay, close your eyes."

He looked at her suspiciously.

"Close your eyes," she said more firmly.

"No," he said equally firmly.

She sighed. "Okay, then." She reached across and took his hand in hers. The expression in his eyes changed instantly and she knew she had him then. "Please, close your eyes, just for a moment. I'll close mine too. Sometimes knowing what you want is easier when you can't see."

"Now you're talking nonsense." But he closed them and she closed hers. "Now, tell me what you like."

"This."

She peeped out of the corner of her eye and saw he was looking at her. "Morgan," she warned.

"This land, I mean, Princess." He looked around.

She opened her eyes. "You like this land? You want your own farm?"

"Not *want*. I'll never have it. But I like it all right. Somewhere where I can breathe, somewhere I can call my own."

"Why is that so important to you?"

He shrugged. "Just is. But it's a dream. And I don't do dreams. I work. I move on."

"Are you running from your past?"

He cocked an amused eyebrow at her. "Fancy yourself an analyst as well as an astronomer?"

"Doesn't take an analyst to see you're running from something. People are either running *to* something, or *from* something. And as we've ruled out that you're running to something, you must be running *from* something. Someone been mean to you, cowboy?"

"Sure have. My stepfather used to give me the bash every time he drank. And he drank all the time."

Rebecca was appalled. "He hit you?"

"Yeah. You think *I'm* a bastard. He really *was* a bastard. Through and through."

"Then why didn't you mother leave him?"

"Too scared. We lived out in the bush behind Hokitika on the west coast. Very remote. Too far to walk to the nearest highway and my mother couldn't drive."

"So how did you get out?"

"I learned how to drive from books, magazines, watching my stepdad. And when I was old enough I drove me and Mum out of there in the old man's clapped-out ute. We disappeared and began a new life with new names. At least until the old man died, a year later. Fell down and broke his leg in the bush. Drunk as a skunk no doubt. And died of exposure so the papers said."

"That's all so terrible!"

"Hell of a relief to us. Mum was able to access some funds then. We both had work and life was good for a few years until Mum passed away. Life with her old man had weakened her."

"So that left *you*. But you had some money inherited from your mother?"

"Yeah, but I didn't want it. I told the lawyers to invest it and left."

"So you were all alone. How old were you when you drove out of the bush?"

He shrugged. "Around twelve I reckon. Not that my birthdays were ever celebrated."

"You drove a car for the first time at twelve?"

"Yep. It wasn't so hard. Not a lot else to do in the bush except watch and learn."

"And you got your first full-time job at twelve?"

"I was big for my age."

"And you lost your mother when you were around fifteen?"

His lips formed a grim line and he swallowed. She stretched out her hand to this man who kept so many secrets, so many painful memories, tight inside. She took his hand in both hers and turned it, looking at it carefully—the hand that had no doubt tried to protect himself from his stepfather's blows, the same hand that had been his mother's savior and that had begun work at such an early age. "I'm so sorry, Morgan. No boy should have to go through experiences like that."

"No boy? No man, no woman and no girl. But people can be cruel. In ways big and small."

There was something in the way he said that which made her wonder if he held more painful secrets locked away in his heart. "I hope no one is ever cruel to you again."

"People can only hurt you if you let them close."

"And you don't do that."

"Not usually. But sometimes... it happens." He brought her hands which still held his, up to his lips and kissed them. "And sometimes, I can't regret it. If there's pain to be had with the closeness, then let it happen. Because there's no going back."

It didn't take much for her to lean over and kiss him. Hardly any movement at all. A foot, half a meter maybe, but once that small gap was bridged, she felt as if she'd floated into a different world.

She fell on top of him, her hands framing his face as her mouth explored his. The slide of her tongue against his was the most sensuous thing she'd ever felt. Her whole attention, her whole being was focused on the connection... in that one place.

It was Morgan who pulled away first. He lifted her off him with ease, as if she weighed nothing. He brushed her cheek with the back of his hand, sliding it down and caressing the only exposed part of her—her neck—before pulling away.

"We're getting to know each other, remember?" he said with a husky growl. "I promised you no sex. And I want you to trust me. Okay?"

She nodded, her body still reeling from the kiss. He

rolled her off and she lay back on the blanket as he looked down at her. The sun was behind his head, illuminating his golden hair with a halo, but hiding his expression. She swept her hand through his hair. "I trust you, cowboy."

He grinned, a cute lop-sided grin and bent down and brushed her lips with his. "Last kiss."

"For today."

He stood up and looked out into the distance. "Time to be getting back."

Rebecca rose gingerly and winced, looking up at her horse with obvious trepidation.

"You okay getting back on?" Morgan asked.

"I'll manage."

But after she got on and her body reminded itself just how uncomfortable she was, she bit her lip and looked at him anxiously. It was enough.

"Okay. You can ride with me and we'll lead your horse."

She would have fallen to the ground as she slithered off the horse, if Morgan hadn't caught her. Once he was back on his own horse he lifted her into his lap and they set off. As the horse fell into a gentle canter, Rebecca leaned against Morgan's chest, her arms wrapped around him, under his coat, and she thought she'd never been so happy.

CHAPTER SIX

Rebecca looked at her watch impatiently. It wasn't yet dark but she'd been ready since mid-afternoon. Ready to show Morgan her world at the Observatory.

She'd only seen him once in the past few days. It had been her day at the Information Office and as she'd approached she'd seen his dog first. As always, Annie was trotting, ears and eyes alert, slightly in front of Morgan, as if checking the way was clear for him.

And as Morgan had turned the corner, the change in his expression made her stomach do somersaults of lust. In that moment she knew she was right to have made the radical alterations to her list which included changing "well-educated" to simply "clever" because that was what Morgan was. He was educated in the ways of the world. And it wasn't even as if she'd had to change some of the items on her list. He was already careful with money. Of course, not *having* any money made that easier.

They'd only exchanged a few words before she went in to work at the Information Center and he'd turned around and went back to his ute. She knew now that

Gemma had been right. Morgan had been making the trip from Glencoe to town on the days she worked just to see her.

And now she was hardly able to wait a few minutes, peeping from behind curtains, turning her music down so she could hear his ute approach. It was totally ridiculous, she told herself as she opened the front door for the third time to see if he was coming. She'd only known him a short time and he was all she could think about.

Then she heard his ute come around the corner accompanied by the familiar excited bark of Annie. Quickly she locked the door and ran down her path just as the ute drew up at the curb. She could feel the dopey grin on her face but she had no way of stopping it as she opened the door and jumped in beside him.

She felt as excited as a kid. *And* as shy. "Hey."

"Hey, you," he smiled. He didn't attempt to drive off.

"How's things?"

"Much better now I'm here. Now"—he reached over and she held her breath as his hand brushed her arm as he reached over for the seat belt—"if you put this on, we can go."

She clicked it into place. "Right. Now, I'll show you the stars."

Darkness was only just beginning to fall as they arrived at the top of Mount John where the two familiar big round domes of the Observatory were sited.

"Have you been up here before?"

Morgan turned a full circle taking in the 360 degree view. He shook his head. "No, never. Amazing view."

Then Rebecca saw them, the tell-tale changes in the

sky. She pointed out toward the horizon. "Not as amazing as this. Looks like we're in for a treat."

As the violet of the sky above darkened, deep magenta columns of light rose from the pale gold horizon, spreading one minute before narrowing like spotlights, shifting like flames. For all its glory, there for anyone to see, it somehow felt intimate, as if the sky was putting on a show just for them. Rebecca couldn't have said how long they stood silently watching the *aurora australis* paint the night sky with its vivid colors, but finally it subsided, settling into a band of bright gold, low on the horizon. And when he reached for her hand it felt completely natural and she curled her fingers into his warm palm until the southern lights had completely faded from the sky.

Neither commented on the lights as they walked toward the Observatory. For once Rebecca was glad Morgan wasn't talkative because it would only have detracted from the beauty of the moment. Morgan opened the door for her and once they were both inside, and her colleagues greeted her, the moment had passed, the magic had gone.

And, Rebecca thought, as she finished showing Morgan around the Observatory, somehow the excitement she usually felt at looking through the huge telescopes, at describing what the different pieces of equipment did, wasn't there. It seemed that all the science in the world couldn't compete with watching the southern lights with Morgan.

Before they left she went into Martin's office.

"Martin," Rebecca greeted him. "Do you remember Morgan? You met him at Violet's christening." She turned to Morgan. "Martin's only been working here a few months."

Martin stood up with a warm smile and extended his

hand to Morgan. "How could I forget Morgan? Apart from anything else he's the man who's put a smile on Rebecca's face."

Morgan frowned slightly and shook the extended hand. "Seems to me she pretty much has a smile most of the time." He glanced at Rebecca and she could tell he was concerned that she'd be embarrassed.

"What can I say? I'm a happy girl."

Martin grinned at Rebecca. "Course you are. Anyway, Morgan, come over here and I'll show you what I've been looking at." Morgan sat in the seat and Martin adjusted the eyepiece. "Comfortable?"

"Sure."

"What can you see?"

"I can see it's Maori New Year."

"New Year? But it's June," said Rebecca.

"When it's Maori New Year, you can see the Great Waka of Tama-rereti in the south."

Martin laughed. "I read up on this for an undergrad paper. The waka is the southern Milky Way." Morgan pulled away from the telescope but Martin didn't move his hand from the back of Morgan's chair.

"Yeah," said Morgan. "And my step-dad told me it contained all of the important stars to navigate by." Morgan paused. "It was the only useful thing he ever told me. Helped me find my way through dense bush as a young 'un."

"I've never found stars useful in a practical sense." Martin smiled.

Morgan gave him a sideways glance. "They're not just useful for navigation. But for animals too. The cattle start getting restless around this time of year. Getting ready for spring and mating."

Martin spluttered out a laugh. "I guess they do." His eyes roamed up and down Morgan's length. "And I guess they're not the only ones." He put his hand on Morgan's arm and Morgan froze, his frown descending once more.

Morgan turned to Rebecca who was checking the telescope's settings. "What else is there to see?"

Startled, Rebecca looked up and wondered why Morgan suddenly appeared uncomfortable. "Well, there's my office and the research I'm doing."

Rebecca introduced Morgan to the others as they passed by, and gave him the run down on some of the projects and the observatory's history. She was talking by rote. She could have given him the spiel in her sleep. It wasn't until they'd entered her office and she'd closed the door that she turned to him.

"What was that all about? Didn't you like looking at the telescopes? What about Hercules, the spectrograph?"

"Of course I did. I've never seen anything like it."

"People usually want to stay there and watch as the universe swings overhead. It's truly beautiful."

"I believe you," he said. He filled the small office. He walked over to the window where the blinds were open. "The stars look pretty good from up here too."

She turned away, and riffled through some papers, trying to hide her confusion. "I'm sorry, I thought you'd find it interesting."

She felt his hands on her arms. "Of course I do. Even if it wasn't your passion, I'd find it interesting. It's part of my life too, you know. Some of those long nights in the bush, when I needed to be away from my stepfather, I'd have been lost without the stars to guide me."

She turned in his arms, not understanding. "Then why did you want to leave Martin so abruptly. Is it because he and I are friends? You think we're in a relationship?"

His lips quirked. "No, Rebecca, that's not what I think."

"I mean, we do have some history."

"Really?"

"There's no need to sound surprised. Some men are interested in me, you know."

"I doubt Martin is."

"And why do you doubt that? Do you think that someone like Martin, good looking, clever, good conversationalist, fun and..." She really couldn't think of anything more to add. "Do you really think someone like him is out of my reach?"

"Frankly, yes."

She pushed away his arms, hurt by his admission that she'd been aiming too high with her pursuit of Martin. "You really have a low opinion of me, don't you?"

He laughed and she swung around, angry now.

"You think I'm so unattractive that someone like Martin wouldn't want to go out with me."

His laughter stopped as suddenly as it started. "You really want to go out with that guy?"

Rebecca half-turned, shrugged and felt her lips turning into an unused position, a pout. "Maybe. We've been out a few times and he, well he's, you know, suitable."

"Ah," sighed Morgan, folding his arms as he leaned back against the window. "You're talking about that damned list of yours, aren't you? Don't tell me, this Martin ticks all the boxes, doesn't he?"

"Well, kind of." *Now* probably wasn't the right time to inform Morgan that she'd changed a few of them since she'd told him about them.

"And tell me, does Martin know all about your plan?"

"No, of course not. We just kind of hung out together. And..." she shrugged.

"And you waited for him to take it to a different level."

"Maybe." She looked up at him shyly.

"Sweetheart..." To her surprise, he sighed and brought her into his arms, and lifted her chin to face him. "It was never going to happen. Sometimes you have to forget the boxes, the ticks, the science behind it all. What did you feel when you were with him?"

It was hard to think at all when she was in Morgan's arms. All her senses focused on the sensations his hands created as they ranged over her back, warming it and sending delicious shivers running through her body. She swallowed and shook her head, unable to think of a single thing. "I don't know."

"It wasn't memorable, then?"

Her breathing was coming too rapid, ratcheting up with each sweep of his hands on her back... and lower. "I guess not."

"He didn't touch you like I'm touching you?"

She opened her mouth to speak, but it was too dry. Nothing came out. She shook her head.

"Any idea why not?"

She frowned, not understanding his question immediately. "I don't know. I guess he didn't like me enough."

"Rebecca." He brushed his finger over her mouth and she opened it, as she tried to press her lips against his finger. But he'd gone before she could. She looked up into his eyes that were dark with desire. "You are adorable." She caught her breath. "How can you be so clever, so knowledgeable about so much, and yet so innocent? Martin was never going to like you enough. You're the wrong sex."

She felt her eyes open wide. "What?"

"He likes men. That much is obvious."

"How? How... how do you know that?"

"For one thing, if he spent time with you and didn't make a pass, there must be something strange going on. There's no heterosexual man on earth who wouldn't want you."

"You're wrong. There are plenty."

"And for another, I know when a man comes on to me."

"You do? How? Has it happened before?"

"When I was a teenager trying to hold down a man's job. When I was young and vulnerable."

"That's terrible."

"I sorted it. These weren't people like Martin. These were men working in a lawless place, used to getting what they wanted. They soon realized I could defend myself. And then I grew a little more and made my preferences clear. I reckon Martin thought he was being subtle."

Rebecca sat down quickly in her office chair. "I've been so stupid!"

He leaned back against the window once more. "Not stupid. Perhaps just overestimated your scientific approach to matchmaking."

"This is so embarrassing. Do you think Martin realized?"

"I doubt it. He probably thought you understood."

She put her hand in her hands. "I still feel stupid."

He walked across the room and looked out the window. "Why don't we go outside? Look at the stars the old-fashioned way?"

"Sure," she said miserably. "I'll get my coat and hat."

He opened the door and she stepped out onto the narrow walkway that circled around the observatory. She shivered and lifted up her collar. It was freezing but the stars in the sky shone like diamonds.

He put his arms around her and she snuggled into them. She still felt stupid. But now she felt warm and stupid. As his hands around her tightened and he pulled her close, she forgot to feel stupid.

"I'm sorry. I wanted to show you around. Show you what my work was all about."

"I doubt I'd have understood it, anyway."

She grunted. "You understand things a lot better than me."

"Maybe I just understand them in a different way."

She sighed and surrendered herself to the pleasure of being engulfed by him—his coat wrapped around her and his arms holding her close.

"I never thought there might be more than one way to understand something. I thought you read about it, thought about it, conducted experiments to see if one's hypothesis was correct, discussed results with colleagues, correlated other people's hypotheses until you came to a result."

She felt the rumble of his laugh against her back. Then she felt the touch of his lips on her hair and she closed her eyes and sighed.

"There are other ways of doing the same thing. When I was a kid I watched what was going on. When I spent the night out in the bush I'd watch the stars, how they'd move, which were the brightest. I listened to other bushmen, I read what I could. I figured out which ones would help me find my way home. Same kind of deal as yours, except fewer books and no computers involved." He paused. "And I reckon you get to know a few things which aren't in books."

"Such as?"

"Some people reckon you can see your future in the stars."

She snorted. "That's nonsense."

"I don't know. I keep an open mind. Not that I want to know my future."

She twisted and looked up at his face, illuminated by only the stars. "You don't?"

He glanced down at her. "No. I might not like it."

She turned back. "Um. Maybe I should try looking for my future in the stars. Seems I'm making a mess of it the conventional way—with lists, with plans, with goals and objectives. If I can't see what's before my eyes—couldn't tell that Martin wasn't the man for me—what hope do I have of sorting out my own future?"

"Let me help." He looked up into the stars. "I reckon you want a regular, predictable kind of life."

"And you can tell that by?"

He pointed out one set of stars. "See Venus over there? She's you. Maori call her *Meremere-tu-ahiahi* because she stands out on the western horizon after the sun sets, bright and beautiful."

She laughed, incredulous. "Is that how you see me? Bright and beautiful?"

"Of course. There's no other way."

There was something glorious about a man who saw her like that, when she saw herself so differently.

"Always there in the early evening, always there in the morning," he continued. "That's how you'd like to be. Nice and predictable and orderly. No shooting stars, or seasonal changes for you."

"Well you're right about the predictable and orderly. Or *was* right. I feel like I've just stepped off that particular ledge."

"And how does it feel?"

"Scary. Like I'm falling."

His grip tightened. "You're not falling. I have you."

She turned around in his arms and her hips met his and she suddenly realized why he'd angled away from her. He didn't want her to know how aroused he was. She swallowed and pulled away. It took all her effort and self-control. "I'm not so sure you having me isn't even more scary."

"I'm sorry. But there's no way I can have you in my arms and not want you."

She nodded and pressed her cheek against his chest. "Me too," she whispered.

He pulled away and she could see a frown on his face. "Tell me, Rebecca, what is it you're so afraid of? You know I'd never do anything to hurt you."

"It's not you I'm afraid of." He bent down and kissed her softly on the lips and her body melted and she sank against him. He pulled away too soon. "It's me. It's my mind I'm afraid of."

"Why would you be afraid of your clever mind?"

"When you kiss me, when my body responds, I stop being clever and I think other things. Except"—she gulped, as she tried to put into words her deepest fears—"except they're not really thoughts, they're needs."

"You're frightened of your body's needs?"

She nodded.

"But that's normal."

She shook her head. "No. I don't think it is. I think... I think"—she squeezed her eyes shut but that didn't stop the tears from running down her cheeks—"I think I have a dirty mind." She gulped. "When I see you, I just want you. I don't care who's about, I don't care if we're seen... in fact I think I'd like it. I just want you. Your body, naked, doing things to me that I can't..."

He groaned and pulled her tight against him. "Rebecca..."

"Morgan, don't you see? I'm so scared of that side of me. I can't believe I'm even saying these things. I've never told anyone before."

"They're natural. It's not dirty. Believe me, I've seen and heard dirty minds talk before and yours comes nowhere close. Besides, it's not like you want to have sex with the whole of Shelter Springs in one session." Then his eyes narrowed anxiously. "Is it?" he added.

She half-spluttered a laugh between the tears. "No. Just you. *All the time*. Just you."

The tension in his face disappeared. "Just me. That sounds good. You can trust me, Rebecca. I'll look after you, make sure you're safe. You can trust me that nothing we do will be dirty. Only good clean, loving fun. Do you trust me?"

She nodded.

"Say it."

"I trust you, Morgan. I trust you like I've never trusted anyone before."

"Good. Then let's go someplace and I'll *show* you that you can trust me."

The journey back to the cottage seemed to take forever. Morgan drove with his arm around Rebecca who nestled into him, her feet curled under her on the seat. She looked at the familiar road in the ute's headlights and felt a sense of wonderment at how unfamiliar it looked. It was as if she'd ventured into new territory.

They pulled up outside her house and the rumble of the ute died into the stillness of the night.

"You okay?" He lifted her chin and kissed her.

"I don't know." It was the only honest answer. She felt she'd gone beyond being okay or not okay. She was simply living in the moment. And she couldn't ever remember having done that before.

He brushed his thumb against her lip. "I want a better answer than that in a little while."

"Like ten minutes?"

His eyes narrowed dangerously. "It'll take me longer than that, sweetheart."

"Half an hour?" she grinned.

"And some."

In the end it was over an hour before they lay, side by side, panting on the bed. "You okay?" he asked.

"Um," she grunted softly. She casually stretched her arm over her face, trying to shelter her reaction. She didn't want him to see her tears. Because how could she explain them when she didn't understand herself?

As the tears flowed down her cheeks, trickled under her chin and onto the sheets, his fingers stroked down her arm, until he reached her hand and enfolded it in his own.

"Rebecca? What's wrong?"

She couldn't speak.

"You surely don't still believe that what we've done is dirty in any way? Because it's not. It's making love."

If he hadn't said those words, she might have got away with the tears. But as soon as he said them, the surge of emotion rose from deep within her and she could hide her tears no longer.

"Ah, Rebecca..." He drew her to him and held her while she cried softly against his chest. He didn't say anything further, just held her, until she'd cried herself out and her breathing had evened out. "Tell me," was all he said.

"I told you I'm adopted. Well, ever since I met my birth mother I've been scared. I'm on the nature side of the nature/nurture debate. I'm a scientist and scientists believe in the laws of science, of genetics, of children being like their birth parents."

"You're frightened of being like your birth parents?"

"Yes, and I've good reason because I know who they are. Or at least... I know what they've done." She swallowed. "When I was fourteen I wanted to know about my birth mother. And I managed to trace her without my parents' help. Turned out they knew more about the circumstances of my birth than they'd ever let on and they wanted to protect me. I didn't find that out until later. At the time, I couldn't understand why my birth mother was reluctant to meet me. Then, when I did meet her, she was cold. She made it very clear that this was to be our one and only meeting and she said that if I had any questions she'd answer them honestly and directly because I wouldn't have another chance."

Rebecca closed her eyes as the memories of that heartbreaking moment consumed her.

"Go on," Morgan prompted gently.

"I asked her a few questions about herself, about me—I can hardly remember them. And then I asked her who my father was. I can picture her now. She was standing by the window, her arms folded, looking out, impatient to leave. I was heartbroken. And when I asked her that question she turned to me and told me that she had no idea who he was. That he'd never been found. I didn't understand. I asked her what she meant by 'found'. She tapped her cigarette into the tray, sucked on it deeply—I remembered that because she was in profile and her nose was exactly like mine. Small, stupid, snub thing."

He kissed her nose. "Nothing stupid about your nose."

She tried to smile but failed and took his hand and rested it across her closed eyes. "And I thought, there, in that moment, in that gesture, this was what I was missing— someone who looked like me, someone to whom I could trace my likes and dislikes, my personality, my looks every- thing. That was what I wanted—to know myself through my birth parents. And despite her attitude I still thought she held the key." She opened her mouth to continue but no sound emerged.

He pulled away his hand and brushed her closed eyes. "Open your eyes and tell me, Rebecca."

She flicked them open and looked into his eyes—eyes that held only her. It gave her the strength she needed. "She said they'd never found the man who'd raped her, who'd left his baby inside her. That by the time she knew she was pregnant, it was too late to get rid of me. Adoption was the only recourse. She had been sixteen, Morgan. What kind of man forces himself on a sixteen-year-old girl?"

He shook his head.

"The answer is a man who couldn't control his base instincts. A cruel man." She inhaled a shuddering breath. "She told me how it happened, what he did to her."

"Why did she put you through that?"

She shrugged. "I think, in some way, she wanted to punish me. Maybe I represented the man who'd raped her... my father. Maybe she wanted to vent a bit on me. Hurt me for how he'd hurt her? I don't know. All I know is that I've never forgotten the terrible details of it. He'd used her again and again."

He swore under his breath.

"That's my father. I carry his genes. I'm terrified I'm some kind of sex maniac like him. When we make love my mind kind of goes blank and I want so much. My body wants yours, in so many ways."

"Rebecca. You're *not* your father, you're *you*. Unique. My birth father was a drunkard and an utter bastard."

"But you know you're nothing like that."

"I have been in the past. But no, I've moved on from that. I trust myself now. Maybe no-one else. But me. And you." He pushed her hair off her face, held her face in both his hands and kissed her. "You're nothing like anyone else. Not your mother who was too cruel in telling you these things. And certainly not your father. He may have been mentally ill, may have been off his head on some drug or other for all you know. None of which has anything to do with you. Do yourself a favor and forget him, forget these things which are haunting you and most probably wrong."

"I can't forget things I know."

"Then don't forget those things, but don't connect them to you. There's no reason to fear your sexuality, simply because you had a rotten father."

There was something in his expression, something so genuine, so loving, something so convincing that it pushed her fears away and she leaned toward him and kissed him.

The kiss turned into something more passionate and they rolled onto the bed and he showed her how totally un-dirty and good loving could be between two people.

. . .

It was still dark when Rebecca awoke to find Morgan dressing. She propped herself on one elbow, patted the table for her glasses and peered at the clock. "Five o'clock! Really?"

"I've slept in. I have to go."

"Breakfast? Toast, coffee?"

"No time." He leaned in and kissed her. "Just time for a kiss." He sighed and swept his hand down her naked body. "Wish I had time for more. But..."

She laughed and jumped out of bed and leaped into his arms. He kissed her again and walked through into the hall and up to the front door. With her still hanging around his neck, kissing his neck, he grabbed his coat from the coat rack and shrugged it on. Then he grabbed her bottom, gave it a good squeeze and a hard kiss and then unceremoniously unpeeled her from him and dropped her to her feet.

He opened the door and a blast of cold air filled the hall. But she didn't dash away, simply stood in her nakedness, her body responding under his lustful gaze and the cold air.

"Thank you, Morgan. Thank you for everything." She reached up once more and kissed him before retreating backward into the hall.

"My pleasure, Princess. I'll see you later." After one last sweeping glance, he closed the door and was gone.

The ute roared into life at the same time as an unfamiliar phone ring tone sounded.

She frowned, pulled on her dressing gown and looked to the floor where a cell phone vibrated. It must be Morgan's. Must have fallen out of his jeans pocket.

"Hello?"

"Who's this? Is Morgan there?"

"Er, no. He's, er, just left."

"Without his phone?"

"Yes. He forgot it."

"Damn." There was silence on the other end of the phone.

"Can I give him a message?"

"Who are you, anyway?"

"I'm..." What on earth was she? "I'm his friend."

"His friend? Right. Like he stays with women friends until five in the morning."

"I really don't see it's any of your business."

"Anyway. Whatever. Just tell him to phone me."

"Who shall I tell him rang?"

"His wife."

CHAPTER SEVEN

"His wife?" repeated Rebecca, the words slowly sinking in.

"That's right. Tell him to ring me. And tell him it's urgent."

Rebecca thought quickly as she tried to suppress the poisonous blend of fear, anger and grief that made her want to vomit. "Urgent?"

"Yes. Tell him we need to talk about Joe."

"Joe?"

"What are you, a parrot or something? Yes, Joe. His son. I guess he didn't tell you about him either." The woman didn't wait for Rebecca to reply. "There's something wrong with him. Morgan needs to ring me as soon as possible."

Rebecca sat down, her legs suddenly weak. She opened her mouth to speak but nothing emerged.

"Did you get that? Urgent."

"Sure." She swallowed. "I'll let him know straight away."

The phone went dead and Rebecca tossed Morgan's phone on the bedcover and stared at it. All the while her mind re-played her night with Morgan, as if she were editing the rushes of a film. His face at the moment she'd climaxed, watching her intently; his thigh muscles, tense as he stood supporting her, her legs wrapped around his hips; his arms holding her as she arched back and thrust herself onto him. She'd let herself go. She'd trusted him, just as he'd told her to. And he'd been deceiving all the time. What else had he lied about?

A cold, calm anger filled her, curbing the deadly hurt. She rose, went into the bathroom and flicked on the shower. While she waited for the water to heat up, she looked at herself in the mirror as the steam rose and curled around her. Her eyes were steady now. She could do this. She'd shower, go find him and give him the message. And then she'd return, have breakfast, check her emails and go to work. Just as she always did. Just, she corrected herself, as she'd always done *before* Morgan.

She had to find that ordered life once more, had to hang on to something solid because Morgan had lied—he'd lured her off her nice, orderly path into chaos with the promise of trust. But she couldn't trust him. And without trust there was nothing.

Once dressed she rang Glencoe but Morgan wasn't there. Apparently he'd gone straight out to a stockyard between the homestead and Shelter Springs.

She jumped in her car and drove through the dark streets, which were only just beginning to lighten. She'd soon left Shelter Springs behind and was approaching the stockyard. Lights spilled out from the open doors of the shed and, as she drew closer, she saw his ute parked outside.

She got out and shivered in the freezing dawn air. One

of the other workers saw her. He called inside: "Boss! You've got company. It's your missus."

Seems like word had got around. Pity word hadn't got around with equal ease that Morgan was already married and that his missus was actually someone else. If she'd known he'd been married, she wouldn't have gone within a mile of him. She didn't do things like that. Being the lover of a married man certainly didn't enter into her future plans.

Before she reached the shed, Morgan appeared. When he saw her, his face lit up. She shook her head in disbelief. How could he look at her like that while he had a wife and son—unacknowledged and needing him?

He raised his arm as if to pull her to him but she stopped short.

"What's wrong?"

She flexed her hands and thrust them into her coat pockets. She didn't know if she was going to punch him or reach for him. "You left you cell phone behind." Her voice rang out sharply across the quiet yard and he narrowed his gaze. She tossed the phone to him and he grabbed it in mid-air.

"You came all this way to give it back? No reason to have done that." He pushed it into his back pocket. "Hardly use it anyway."

"*You* might not, but someone called you."

He frowned. "Callum? But he knew I'd be here."

"Not Callum. Your wife."

"What?"

She cleared her throat. "Your wife rang. She asked me to pass on a message to you that Joe's sick. That your child, your *son*, is sick."

"Joe? What's wrong with him?"

Until his reply, Rebecca hadn't realized that she'd been

waiting for Morgan to deny it all, to tell her that it must be the wrong number, or that it was all lies. In weak moments on the drive over she'd figured that maybe this was all some mad ex's figment of her imagination. But in that moment, when he hadn't even attempted to deny it, the anger ebbed away, evaporating like a mist burned to nothing by the sudden blast of the mid-summer sun, and the tears emerged. She bit her lip. She *would* not cry.

"Your wife didn't share the details with me. She just wanted me to tell you as soon as possible. And I've done that so I'm going." Rebecca turned to leave but Morgan was too quick and grabbed her arm, stopping her in her tracks. She couldn't look into his face, simply stared at his fingers that sunk into her thick coat. She could feel their strength through the layers, burning her skin. "Take your hands off me!"

"No, I need to know what she said. Did she say where she is? Where Joe is?" He walked in front of her, his hands gripping her arm more tightly still. "Did she say anything about where they were?"

She tried to wriggle out from under his firm grip but he wasn't letting her go.

"Rebecca, was there anything else? Anything at all?"

"There was *nothing* else. Why don't you damn well ring her and ask her if you're so anxious?"

He took his phone and scanned the recent calls and pressed dial. "You don't understand."

"Morgan, I understand the facts perfectly. That's what I do for a living. I examine things, I draw conclusions. It's not that hard. Now, I'm sure you've things to sort out, so I'll be leaving."

"Wait! Rebecca, just wait and I'll explain—"

Rebecca glanced at him but someone had obviously

responded on the other end of the phone and Morgan had stopped mid-sentence and turned away from her. And in that moment, with his back to her, as he spoke the name of the woman to whom he was married she felt a fresh blast of grief, that shattered her anger. The tears began to fall before she turned and walked away, before Morgan could see. They began to fall in earnest as she started the car and she was driving blind by the time she turned onto the country road, back to her home, back to her life before Morgan.

***

Where was she? Morgan stepped back over the low fence at the back of Rebecca's cottage and cursed softly as the curtains twitched at a neighbor's property. He'd be had up for trespassing next.

He knocked once more on the back door, trying to see any movement through the kitchen window. But there was none. No lights, no radio, no movement, no sign of life. All the other windows still had their heavy curtains drawn against the night. But it was no longer night and it was obvious that Rebecca hadn't returned home from the stock-yard. It was eight in the morning and he couldn't find here anywhere.

She wasn't at the Observatory, she wasn't answering her home or cell phone, and it didn't look as if she was at home. Her car wasn't outside for one thing and, for another, her paper and mail were still stuffed in the letterbox. She'd have cleared them if she'd been home. He'd tried Gemma but she didn't know where she was either. It seemed she'd vanished into thin air.

Damn Leah. He got into his ute and made a few detours hoping he'd find Rebecca walking or driving through the quiet streets of Shelter Springs. But no such luck and after a few circuits of the small town, he'd returned to the road to Glencoe. If she didn't want to see him there wasn't much he could do about it. But there was something else he definitely needed to do. He needed to track down his son. He needed to see the only person he could think of who might be able to help.

Morgan found Callum in his office. He'd looked everywhere else first because he knew that Callum would rather be outside doing something than stuck indoors at a desk. He understood the scowl on Callum's face.

He knocked on the open door.

Callum turned around and the scowl disappeared. "Morgan! Come in."

Morgan walked into the book-lined study and nodded in greeting. "Do you have a few minutes?"

"Certainly do. I'm glad of the break. All this"—he indicated a pile of scattered papers on his desk—"legal stuff to do with the settlement of the estate is driving me mad." He sighed and stood up. "So what's up? Anything wrong down at the sheds?"

"No, it's all good. Just wanted a word about another matter—something personal—if you've time."

Callum nodded thoughtfully. "Coffee?"

"Thanks."

"Take a seat."

Morgan walked past the leather suite and coffee table and sat on one of the hard-backed chairs at the meeting table.

Callum brought two black coffees to the table. "Here you go. So tell me what's on your mind."

That was one of the many things Morgan respected about Callum. He didn't mess around, didn't talk for the sake of it. They even liked the same drink. Black coffee. No sugar.

"I need help. I know you have contacts in the States and I'm asking for help to find someone."

"Who?"

"My child." He paused. "And his mother."

To Callum's credit all he did was raise his eyebrows and take another sip of coffee. Then he sat back and eyed him directly. "Sure. Give me the details and I'll give my contacts a call."

Half an hour later and Callum's contacts were able to reassure Morgan that they'd be able to find Leah and Joe, in whatever way they needed to—legal or illegal.

"Take the rest of the day off. Sort your stuff out. By the end of the day, unless Leah is cleverer than I imagine, we'll have an address and you can get yourself out there."

"Thanks." Morgan tried to think of something else to say, something that would better express his feelings of relief. He'd thought he'd find it difficult asking someone— especially Callum, because of who he was, a Mackenzie and owner of Glencoe—for help. But Callum had made it easy for him. And Morgan felt nothing but relief. Words floated into his mind and fell away again. He rose. "Thanks," he repeated. "I appreciate it."

Callum nodded to Morgan in acknowledgement as he began talking on the other end of the phone. Morgan closed the door behind him. But instead of returning to his quarters, he went to the ute. Packing could wait. He needed to see Rebecca before he left. But he needed to find her first.

After spending the morning driving to Christchurch only to get there and decide to turn back, Rebecca had arrived at the Observatory six hours later just in time to begin work. She felt exhausted but calm until she entered her office to find Morgan sitting silently opposite Martin who was talking ten to the dozen. Morgan jumped up as soon as she entered.

"Rebecca!"

Martin turned around to see her. "At last, the mystery is solved! Miss Mayhew hasn't been abducted by aliens after all. Morgan"—he turned with a grin to Morgan—"I shall leave you in her capable hands."

"Please stay, Martin," Rebecca said frostily, trying to calm the violent beating of her heart. "We don't need privacy, do we Morgan?" She stared at him, daring him to contradict her.

"Oh, no, my dear, I'm out of here," said Martin quickly.

"Stay!" she said too fiercely.

Martin's eyes widened but he stayed. He pulled a face and held up his hands in surrender. "Fine, I've some emails to check." He sat down with his back to them and waved his hand. "Just carry on as if I'm not here."

"Rebecca, I..." Morgan glanced helplessly at Martin.

"I'm not sure why you came Morgan, but I really don't see there's anything to talk about and, as you see, I'm at work and need to get on. So..."

"I'm not leaving."

Martin glanced up at Morgan who seemed larger than usual in the small office she and Martin shared. Then Martin glanced back at Rebecca. "He's not leaving, you know. I'd get it over with if I were you."

She could see by Morgan's implacable stance that Martin was right.

"Okay. So did you find your son?" she asked frostily.

"Son?" exclaimed a shocked Martin.

"Yes, son. Apparently Morgan has a wife and child." She was talking to Martin, but looking directly at Morgan.

Martin looked up at Morgan. "For real?" He swore under his breath. "I'm out of here. A small scene I can cope with but this could be too dramatic even for me." With that, he'd disappeared out the door before Rebecca could react.

Truth was, she'd forgotten about Martin. She could only focus on Morgan and trying to suppress the wave of pain that threatened to overwhelm her. She swallowed and gulped in a quick breath.

"Rebecca, I..."

"How's your family?" she interrupted. "Well, I hope?"

"Rebecca, don't do this. Let me explain."

"Explain?" She shrugged and walked over to her computer, focusing on forcing her shaking fingers to press the right keys. "You don't have to explain anything to me— an *ex* girlfriend." She sat down and swiveled the mouse around the desk to activate the cursor. "Maybe I wasn't even a girlfriend. Perhaps I had some other name which I don't know. Because I don't know how to play this game, Morgan."

"It's no game. This is about my son. I need to find him."

"You shouldn't have lost him in the first place."

His grip was savage against her arms as he jerked her to standing. "Don't be so damned flippant. You don't know *what* you're talking about."

She twisted her arms free and slammed her hands against his chest—twice. "Of course I don't. Why? Because you've told me nothing. Nothing!"

He reached out to her. "That's what I'm trying to do now. Honey, I—"

She slapped back his hand. "Don't you dare 'honey' me." She paced away, glaring at him all the while.

He held up both hands as if trying coax a reluctant mare.

"And don't do that hand thing to me that you do with horses. I'm not a damn horse."

"Just listen to me."

"Why should I? I'm not your wife."

"My wife never listened to me anyway." He thrust his hands in his pockets and looked at her ruefully.

"So you admit that she's your wife, then. *That* wasn't a figment of my imagination."

"She *was* my wife. *Was*. Past tense. She's not my wife any longer. We're divorced. For a couple of years."

"Come on a minute. Someone's lying here. Why should I believe you, and not your wife?"

"It's up to you who you believe. But I thought you'd know me better than that, know that I wouldn't lie to you."

"But you didn't tell me about your ex-wife, or about your child. Do I have to ask you specific questions to get the full picture from you?"

"I'd have told you about Joe at some point but it's hard talking about him. I don't talk about Joe, I don't talk about Leah, to anyone. I don't *want* to talk about Leah and Joe... it hurts. But I would have told you."

"And why aren't you with them? A father should be there for his child."

"Don't you think I want to be? Look, it's not that easy." He paused. "It's complicated."

"Of course it is," she said with heavy sarcasm.

"You don't understand, Rebecca."

"And how can I if you don't tell me anything?"

"I'll tell you now. Anything. What would you like to know?"

She suddenly felt exhausted and sat back on her chair. "I'd like to know about your marriage and your son. Everything."

"Then I'll tell you."

There was a knock at the door and Martin peered around. "Everything okay?" Without waiting for an answer he placed two coffees on the desk. "Rebecca, you look dreadful, have a coffee." He glanced at Morgan. "And *you* don't look dreadful at all, even if you should. But you can have a cup anyway."

Neither of them acknowledged Martin—they only had eyes for each other—as he quickly left the room.

Morgan sighed and sat down opposite her. "I'm sorry you found out like this. She texts me from time to time. It's usually about money. She always claims it's urgent and it never is, so I've stopped responding."

"She depends on you for money?"

"I doubt I'm her only source of income."

"Another man, you mean?"

"She's had plenty of them since we've separated. Even before we separated. And no doubt plenty since we've divorced. But they're not all such a soft touch when it comes to giving her money."

"And why are you?"

He took a sip of scalding coffee and then placed it on the table, absent-mindedly spooning in a couple of spoon-fuls of sugar. Rebecca knew for a fact that Morgan didn't take sugar. "Because of Joe. It's all I can do to help him."

"Why?"

"Because she won't tell me where they are." He sighed and she could see the pain etched in the lines around his mouth. And when he looked up, in the sadness in his eyes. "She just upped and left with Joe two years ago. I think she's in the States. But no idea which city. It'll be a big city, somewhere with a lot of illegal immigrants. Somewhere she can blend in."

"Why won't she tell you where they are? Why doesn't she want you to know? I don't understand. What's she scared of?"

"It's all a game to her. She's always been a drama queen creating rifts, petty arguments, to keep herself amused. The more desperate she thinks I am to see Joe, the more determined she is not to tell me. She seems to think I stole her youth, getting her pregnant at eighteen. And five years later she's still trying to punish me."

"Then why doesn't she let you have Joe?"

"Because she loves him. I know she loves him and so far I'm guessing he hasn't interfered with her private life. I reckon the day he gets in the way of what she wants to do is the day she'll tell me where they are."

"Do you think that day's come?"

"Maybe. Seems something's bad happened to Joe. Some kind of trauma. I don't really know. Leah was vague but I think she's panicking. But not enough to tell me where they are. Just enough to demand money."

"What do you think's happened to him?"

He shook his head. "I don't know. All I could get out of her was that it wasn't life-threatening."

"Is there any other way you can find them? Can't you get her traced? Won't the police help?"

"No. I've tried everything I could think of. I've gone to lawyers to see if I could get custody, or get information in exchange for child support. I've even hired private detectives but they didn't come up with anything. So I've gone to

Callum. His family have contacts in the States and it looks like they can help—one way or another."

He took a sip of his sweet coffee and grimaced. She pushed over hers and, unaware of what he was doing, he drank it back.

"I'm worried about Joe," he continued. "Leah says he's not going to school and won't let her out of his sight. She reckons she can't work and that's why she needs money. Worries the hell out of me. Health care is expensive in the States. I told her to come back here and get him treated but she won't."

"Maybe there's nothing much wrong with him," said Rebecca, beginning to form a picture of Leah. "And you can't trust what she says, can you?"

"No way. But I can't dismiss it either. Even if Callum's contacts draw a blank I'm going to the States to try to track them down." He rubbed his eyes with the heel of his hands and stared out at the night sky littered with stars.

She followed his gaze and saw once more the universe with his eyes—chaotic and magical. She looked back at Morgan. "Tell me about Joe."

He bit his lip but continued to look into the night sky. "He's just had his fifth birthday. He's a good boy. Just as well with a mother like Leah. He's a bit on the serious side but he's brave. When she's feeling generous Leah'll put him on the phone and I can talk to him. I just hate..." He pressed his lips together and took another sip of the over-sweet coffee, without noticing he didn't like it. "I hate the thought that he's not happy, that he's sick, that he's missing me, wondering where I am. And I hate the thought that she's shacked up with someone who might hurt him."

How had it happened, she wondered? That she could actually feel such empathy for someone, that she could feel his pain viscerally, greater than her own. She choked back tears but this time, they weren't for herself, but for him. She reached over and placed her hand on his. "You'll find him, don't worry." She paused and withdrew her hand. "What will you do once you find him?"

"I'm done trying to talk to Leah. It's time for me to bring him home. I need to get back. See if there's any news. Try to find out where they are."

They both rose and she took his cup from him. She wanted to reach out for him, she wanted to connect with him, to break down that barrier that had arisen between them. But he had things to do—family to track down—that had nothing to do with her. She suddenly had an image of him on a path to her, a path where they'd collided intensely for one short period of time, before he'd glanced off and gone careening away from her. All the time her instincts were screaming at her to reach out for him, she knew she couldn't, not if she were to protect herself. And who would look after her if she didn't? "Good luck."

He nodded once and then left.

She remained standing looking at the closed door, listening to his retreating footsteps before they were lost in the noise of the observatory. "Right." She turned away and logged onto the computer, willing her fingers to move over the keyboard, willing her mind to turn away from that place of pain that she felt as if it were a physical thing, and take control once more.

CHAPTER EIGHT

Three weeks later...

Morgan peered out the airplane window, searching through the white fluffy clouds that floated beneath them for the first signs of the sweep of the South Island coastline. His eyes were scratchy and tired—he felt like he hadn't slept in a week, and he probably hadn't—but he couldn't stop looking until he'd seen it. He didn't think he'd ever wanted to see anything so much. Three weeks away from his country, his land, his home, and he couldn't wait to return.

But it wasn't just about him. He couldn't wait to show Joe his new home. He looked at the sleeping boy whose head lay in his lap, his small body curled under the blanket. Joe had managed to stay awake for much of the flight but now, just when they were about to land, he was dead to the world.

He placed his hand—which covered most of Joe's back—on top of him gently, needing to feel the heat of his small body, to make it real. He knew it wasn't going to be easy—

his son was withdrawn and uncertain—but he also knew there could be no other outcome. He'd found his son and he was never going to let him go. And he'd make sure he grew up without the hang-ups that he had.

It had only been after they'd boarded the flight back to New Zealand that Morgan had had time to think things through, to wonder how he was going to cope with a young boy as a solo dad. Up until then he'd had no thought beyond his need to take his son home with him. The weeks had passed in a whirlwind series of meetings—hysterical ones at first with his ex when she'd discovered he wouldn't be giving her the money that she'd wanted to buy a car to go around the States with her new boyfriend and Joe. But the hysteria had quietened when Morgan had given her a vision of what her life could be like *without* Joe. A life where she could come and go as she pleased.

Seems he'd always frustrated her by his lack of reaction to her dramatics... until the day she'd taken Joe away. But that feeling of satisfaction had been short-lived and she'd soon discovered how having a small son cramped her style. And when she was offered her freedom again, she'd grabbed it with both hands.

Morgan liked to think Leah loved Joe, he liked to believe that Leah realized that Joe would be better off with him than with the men she liked to hang out with. And he'd made sure that Leah knew that she could visit Joe any time she was in New Zealand. But he also made sure she realized that he wouldn't be returning to the States.

Just then the clouds parted and the white surf-edged coastline of the South Island became visible. Morgan gave a deep sigh of relief. Then the landing announcement was made.

He bent down. "Joe," he whispered.

"Um," came the sleepy rumble.

"Look, out the window. It's New Zealand. We're almost home."

Joe propped himself up on one hand and peered sleepily out the window. Then he got excited and knelt before it, his finger tracing the white-fringed coastline of New Zealand. "Is that Christchurch?" he said pointing to the sprawl of buildings on the plain.

"Yes."

"Wow, are they the mountains you told me about?"

"The Southern Alps. Or *Ka Tiritiri o te Moana* as Maori call them."

"They're awesome," he said with his American accent.

"And you see the highest one? That's Aoraki, or Aorangi, who was a person."

"A real person?" Joe's eyes widened.

"He's real in Maori tradition. The story went that he and his brothers were in a canoe which wrecked. And he scrambled to the highest point of the canoe's upturned hull. So that's him we're looking at."

Morgan had to contain a smile at Joe's disbelieving expression.

"And you live in the mountains?"

"Close by. You'll like it. There are lots of animals—horses, cows, sheep, even llamas."

"Cool."

"And my dog, Annie."

"You've got a dog?"

"Sure have. Goes everywhere with me."

"Mum wouldn't let me have a dog. But there was one that used to come around the trailer at nights and I used to feed it after Mum went to bed."

Morgan's heart contracted a little at the image Joe's few

words created in his mind. "I reckon you could do with a dog of your own."

"For real?" Joe began jumping up and down excitedly, squealing. Morgan tried to calm the over-tired, over-excited little boy down, all the while thinking that there was more to this parenting lark than he'd first imagined. In the end it wasn't anything Morgan did that stopped the boy. White-faced, Joe suddenly stopped, his mouth trembling. "I feel sick."

Morgan fumbled, too late, for a sick bag.

Outside the terminal building, Morgan hitched the now sleeping Joe higher onto his hip and looked around. Callum had said he'd have a ute available for him to use but there'd been no keys waiting for him at the airport. Then he saw him.

Callum walked around the building and nodded at Morgan in his typically understated way. Morgan nodded back.

"You got the little fella, then."

"Yep. Leah didn't need much persuading."

"Let me take your bag." Callum approached and grimaced. "You stink."

"Yeah, I know. Joe was sick." He looked ruefully down his shirt which had caught the full impact of Joe's vomit. "Got through Customs pretty quick, though," he grinned. "One whiff and the crowds parted."

"You got anything to change into?"

"In my bag. Haven't had a chance yet."

"Here, give the lad to me."

Joe didn't wake while he was transferred to Callum. Morgan swiftly pulled off the soiled shirt, oblivious to the stares of passing women, and pulled on a t-shirt from his bag. He stuffed the soiled shirt at the bottom. "Cheers, mate." He took Joe back again. "So where's the ute?"

"No ute. I brought the plane. Thought you both might appreciate a quicker journey back.

"Thanks."

Callum Mackenzie was a good man, Morgan thought as they walked to Callum's plane. Before he'd come to Glencoe he'd never have imagined Callum would be like that, and he still had a hard time coming to terms with it. But he sure appreciated his generosity now.

They were soon taxiing down the runway. Joe remained fast asleep in Morgan's arms. Morgan looked at him and yet again felt a wave of pure love pass through him. It was becoming familiar to him now and he knew he'd never be able to live without it again.

He turned to see Callum had been watching him. "You going to stay on a bit longer at Glencoe?"

"No. Joe needs to be close to the city, for doctors, school, friends. And I need help looking after him when I'm away."

"You could have that at Shelter Springs."

"I've other reasons, too, for leaving. It's time to move on."

Morgan looked down at the mountain pass that led from the plains into the high pastures of the Mackenzie country in silence.

"Gemma says she's happy to help out as much as she can. Her being at home with the baby and all."

"That's good of her. But I wouldn't want to impose. And, as I say, it's time to move on."

"You wouldn't be imposing, and why not accept her offer? At least until you've sorted yourself out."

Morgan looked at Callum, who was grinning. "I'm not going to have a say in it, am I?"

Callum shook his head. "No way."

They fell into companionable silence as the miles slipped away and the lands of Glencoe were revealed beneath them. First up were the merino sheep, brought down from the high snowy pastures into the fenced corrals closer to the homestead. And then the estate buildings came into view, with Glencoe homestead, grand and central behind the lake. It was a world within a world. Like a small country, Morgan thought. And within that small country was a woman who hadn't left his mind in all the time he'd been away.

"Seen much of Rebecca?" Morgan asked in what he hoped was a casual voice. But from Callum's twist of the lips, he didn't think he'd managed it.

"She was at Glencoe when I left."

"Right."

"Don't know if she's still there though. Gemma reckons she's pretty cut up about things."

Morgan winced and looked out the window, hating the thought of how much he'd hurt Rebecca.

"Personally, I reckon some crawling on your part is in order."

"Hmph! Crawling? I'd do more than that if I thought it'd make a difference. But I reckon I've stuffed things up good and proper with her."

"I'm not so sure."

"I am." He sighed. "She's a woman who knows her own mind and it's a fierce mind at that. I've a feeling that once she's made up her mind that I'm not to be trusted there's nothing that will change it."

"You could try."

He could, Morgan thought to himself. He could.

Rebecca was about to get into her car when Morgan and Callum rounded the corner of the house. They were early. As soon as she'd heard the sound of the plane entering the valley she'd handed Violet back to Gemma and grabbed her bag. She *couldn't* see him. She didn't *want* to see him. But Gemma had stalled her with various excuses making her unable to leave before they'd arrived.

She gripped the keys to her car tightly and held them up by way of explanation. "I was just leaving."

Morgan ignored what she was saying and approached her with Joe in his arms, wrapped in a blanket which Callum had thoughtfully brought with him. "It's good to see you."

She swallowed and nodded, unable to trust herself to answer. Luckily, at that moment, Gemma appeared—passed a sleeping Violet to Rebecca who could do nothing but accept her—and pushed down the blanket so she could see Joe's face. "Is he okay?"

"Yeah. Just tired. Got sick on the plane coming into Christchurch."

"Here, give him to me and I'll take him to his room."

Morgan looked over to his worker's cottage. "His room?"

"You don't think I'd let you take him to your cottage, do you? No," Gemma continued, not waiting for Morgan to respond. "No, you'll both stay with us in our guest room until we can come up with a better arrangement."

Callum passed Morgan's bag to Maria, the housekeeper. "Better take it to the guest room which you've no doubt prepared."

"But... but you have your family staying," Morgan remonstrated. "I don't want to inconvenience you."

"It's no inconvenience," Gemma replied firmly. "We have eight bedrooms, may I remind you. Plenty of room for everyone. Besides, it'll give us all a chance to get to know Joe. And Maria and I will help you look after him when you need to be out on the estate."

Rebecca could see he was relieved. "I'm grateful for your help over the next few days. But I won't be staying."

"Well, promise me you'll stay at least for a few weeks. Give Joe a chance to recover."

Morgan hesitated.

"For Joe?" Gemma added.

Morgan nodded. "Sure. Thank you."

Despite all the talking to herself Rebecca had done over the past few weeks, she couldn't help feeling hope stir inside her. She'd thought she'd buried it. She'd thought wrong.

Gemma looked at him with a smug expression as though she'd always known she'd get the outcome she wanted. Then she looked back at the sleeping boy. "Poor kid. Leave him with me and I'll call you when he wakes up." Gemma turned to Rebecca. "Becks?"

"I'm just leaving."

"Not with my baby, you're not. Come back inside and have some lunch." But before Rebecca could give Violet back to her parents, Gemma and Callum had disappeared into the house.

Morgan grinned at Rebecca. "You've been outmaneuvered."

Rebecca looked down at Violet, not wanting to get caught in Morgan's gaze. "Looks like it."

"It's good to see you, Rebecca."

She bit her lip, took a breath, tried to think of one of the million retorts that she'd practiced over the past few weeks, but drew a blank. She sighed. "I need…"

"Yes?"

"To get Violet inside. She should go into her cot."

Morgan nodded and together they walked up the steps and into the house in silence. By the time they entered the grand hall of the homestead, there was no sign of Gemma, Callum or the housekeeper. There was an awkward pause. Morgan looked around uneasily, obviously unused to the grandeur of the front entrance. He looked tired. Still gorgeous, of course, but exhausted. She couldn't keep the defensive anger in place any longer and her heart went out to him.

"So… how was it?"

He turned to face her as if surprised by her sudden question. He shrugged. "Difficult."

"To find them?"

"No. Thanks to Callum, that bit was easy. And even getting Leah to agree was easier than I thought. But all the paperwork, the lawyers, all that stuff, I'm not used to that. *That* was hard."

"But you got there in the end."

"Yeah, I got there in the end. Thank God." A chill blast of air suddenly came in through the open door and her hair flicked across her face. He reached forward and pushed it back behind her ear. "It's good to be home." He looked surprised at his own words. "Back in New Zealand, I mean."

"It's good to…" She stopped herself just in time. "I mean I'm glad it worked out for you." She cleared her throat. "Gemma has some lunch ready for you. Are you hungry?"

At that moment a boy's sleepy voice could be heard from up in one of the bedrooms. "That would be nice.

But"—he shot a look upstairs—"I'd better go and check on Joe."

Rebecca watched him take the stairs two at a time, anxious to get back to his son. His son, about whom she knew nothing. That road down which Morgan had gone, leaving her, didn't seem to be circling back to her at all. He seemed more distant than ever.

Rebecca turned to find Maria, the housekeeper, standing with outstretched arms. She gave her the baby and wandered into the drawing room where Gemma and the housekeeper had laid out lunch to welcome back Morgan and Joe. She left the food untouched and wandered over to the window. Seeing Morgan again had exploded her emotions and had sent her thoughts into a state of confusion once more. She'd wanted to run into his arms as soon as she'd seen him. But the feelings of anger and disappointment still lingered and she'd stayed put. Even if she'd ever get over them, what then? He would be leaving soon. There was no future with him.

And then there was Joe. He was the spitting image of Morgan but there was undoubtedly a mark of his mother there too. And Rebecca felt an unfamiliar blast of jealousy.

No matter what lies she'd told herself, she'd come to Glencoe to see Morgan who obviously couldn't wait to leave her. And she'd come to help Joe. But he didn't need her either. He had Gemma who, since Violet's birth, had become exceedingly motherly. And he had Morgan who seemed instinctively to know what to do. Fat lot of use she was going to be. Unless someone needed to know how nuclear fusion explains how stars shine, she was going to be of no help whatsoever. For once in her life she felt lost. She was in a situation in which no amount of theorizing would give her the right answer. She had to try a different method, and she hadn't a clue what. And why bother anyway? He'd be gone soon. A few days... a few weeks? It hardly mattered when the outcome would be the same. He'd be gone from her and she'd stay on here, alone... and lonelier than before.

She watched some of the estate workers doing some maintenance work on the trees and gardens around the lake, preparing for next month's ice-skating party—one the Mackenzies held every year on their lake. She'd been looking forward to it. It was usually fun. She loved ice-skating and she'd enjoyed the event in previous years. But she'd hardly given it a thought this year. Would Morgan still be here for it? If he agreed to Gemma's suggestion, and it looked like he would, she might have a few weeks with him.

A few weeks. The thought of time with him filled her with pleasure despite herself. *A few weeks.* If that was all she had with him, then why not follow her instincts and enjoy them? There would be nothing more... no future for them. He was determined to move away and she never would. He was a drifter, a loner and she needed order in her life. They were poles apart, not destined to be together, but... she had these few weeks.

At that moment the door opened and Morgan stood there, looking tired but as strong and dependable as ever. She jumped up and only just stopped herself from rushing over to him.

"Your coffee's here."

He held his hat uncertainly, not moving. "This is Lady Mackenzie's drawing room."

"She's not here. And Gemma reckons it has too nice an outlook to keep it for Lady Mackenzie's exclusive use. Besides Gemma can't stand her." She walked up to him, took his hat and placed it on the sideboard and passed him a coffee. "I wouldn't worry. Lady Mackenzie is a terrible old snob. She's been as mean as heck to Gemma. I reckon she deserves a little disrespect."

His face tilted into a brief smile. "Reckon you're right there."

But he still didn't sit down in one of the over-stuffed chairs. He stood by the window and knocked back a coffee and ate a couple of sandwiches.

"You're hungry."

"It's not easy to eat with a kid either jumping around you, or asleep on your lap."

"Must have been difficult to adjust to."

"Not really. It's what I dreamed of for years."

She just managed to stop herself from bridging the gap between them and touching him on the arm, making a connection. She swallowed. "I'm glad it worked out for you."

He looked down at her. "It's just the beginning. I know it won't be easy but I'll make it work."

She felt a shadow of sadness that Morgan would make something work for his son, but not their relationship. She nodded and stepped away. "Do you want another coffee?"

"No." He looked around like a caged animal. "What I'd like to do is get out of here." He looked around at the portraits that hung around the wall. Above the grandly carved fireplace, replete with gilt frame, hung a picture of Sir Hugh Mackenzie, Callum, Dallas, and James's father. Morgan's roving eyes stopped on the portrait. Sir Hugh Mackenzie was standing in a commanding position with Glencoe as the backdrop. Morgan walked up to the portrait and stood frowning before it.

Rebecca came up behind him. "That's Callum's dad. Wasn't such a nice man by all accounts." She was puzzled by Morgan's fascination. "Gemma says that there would be no Glencoe, no properties in Wellington where Dallas and Cassandra and their family live, no wealth at all, if it hadn't been for Dallas in the first instance and then the other brothers stepping up and saving their inheritance. And not only saving it but increasing it. Sir Hugh Mackenzie nearly lost it all."

"And yet there he stands, as if he has the world at his feet."

"I think he did. *Then*, anyway. His grandfather had built up quite an empire."

"Which this man"—Morgan nodded dismissively at the portrait—"frittered away."

"In just about every way he could. From what Gemma's told me, he had a drinking problem among other things. He hated Cassandra's father and took over his company, which led to an awful tragedy for Cassandra. No, not a nice man at all." He turned slowly to her, the portrait hanging directly behind him. She looked from one to the other and frowned.

"You worry about your genetic inheritance, Rebecca. Look at Sir Hugh Mackenzie's sons—Dallas and Callum— they're good men. Not like their father at all."

She nodded. "James is too."

"Hmph!" He turned away.

"Don't you like James?"

"I don't like the way he looks at *you*."

She took a step closer to him, unable to prevent a small smile. She knew she shouldn't, but she liked this possessive Morgan. "And which way is that?"

His eyes narrowed. "Like all he has to do is smile that charming smile of his and you'll go running to him."

"And did he smile?"

Morgan grunted and looked away. "You know he did."

She shrugged, looking innocent. "And did I go running?"

He looked back at her. There was a moment's pause. "No, you didn't."

"And doesn't that tell you anything?"

"That you're too damn clever to get sucked in by the likes of him."

With every word, every movement, every jealous instinct of his, he was telling her what she wanted to know, what he refused to tell her in words.

Every instinct in her screamed to go up to him, to touch his arm, to mold her palm to his muscles on which the sunlight from the open window played, causing shadows that only accentuated his strength. She'd shift her hand then, not to the rest of his body, as much as she'd like to, but to his face. To hold it between her hands and to stand on tip-toe, while at the same time she'd pull him down and kiss him. She wanted to do this so she could *know* him again, so she could feel his breath in her mouth and forget all the problems, all the hurdles that lay between them. Even if it was for a short time.

She wanted to do these things. But she didn't. She was too unsure, too scared that she'd make a fool of herself, that Morgan didn't want *her* as much as *she* wanted him.

"Would you like anything else to eat?" She walked briskly over to the table. "Gemma had the housekeeper bake some pies she thought you'd like."

She turned and he stood immediately behind her. She was so close she could see the dark flare of desire in his eyes. He flexed his hands and shook his head.

"No, I want to be with Joe when he wakes up. I need to make sure he settles in okay."

She nodded, her heart about to break. "Settle into New Zealand. But—"

"Not settle into Glencoe. That's right. It's not his home. I need to be nearer town, for Joe's sake. I want to get him into school and stay put until he's finished. It's too remote for him out here."

"But Gemma and Callum's kids will be here," remonstrated Rebecca.

"And they have the money to move around whenever, to wherever they like. I need to find a place where Joe can mix with kids and have a normal life. Where I can find someone who can look after Joe while I'm working. I need to put down roots."

She frowned. "And you can't put them down here? Shelter Springs has a school. There'll be people who can help. Me, for instance."

"You work full time, sometimes shift work. And you're not his mother."

She bit her lip, trying to prevent the hurt and the words springing to her lips that she didn't dare utter. "No," she mumbled awkwardly, "I'm not." She turned away.

"I mean... Just that he's my responsibility, not yours."

"Sure. I get what you mean." She smiled what she hoped was a confident and reassuring smile but if it revealed a small part of how she felt, she knew she'd have failed.

"I can't stay here." He paced away, glanced up at the portrait. "It's this place," he looked around, as if in despair. "It's not for me."

"It's just a place, Morgan."

"It's more than that. I can't explain."

"Try."

He opened his mouth as if to speak but closed it again. "I can't. It's not right. You'll have to take my word for it."

A month ago and she'd have argued with him, would have tried to see the logic in his argument, tried to win him over with her own reasoning. But instead she nodded her head, as she tried to fight the urge. She felt more for Morgan than she'd ever felt for anyone and she knew that throwing words at this cowboy wasn't the way to win him over. There was only one way to do that... and that was with actions. Just what she could do though, she had no idea.

The door opened and Gemma put her head around. "Joe's awake and he wants you." Gemma smiled uncertainly at Rebecca as she took a step forward too. "I think he might just want his dad, Rebecca."

"Oh..." Rebecca stopped and looked at Morgan.

"Just for now," Gemma added gently. "He'll be more settled tomorrow."

Rebecca went into the hall with Gemma and watched Morgan climb the grand staircase feeling the distance between them grow even more.

Gemma put an arm around her and gave her a brief hug. "It'll be all right, Becks. Joe's just unsettled and I don't blame him. He'll be fine in a few days. But for now, I think he's best off with his dad."

Rebecca watched Morgan disappear. Joe might be fine, but what about Morgan... what about her?

CHAPTER NINE

Morgan stood outside Rebecca's door, his hand poised to knock. But he hesitated. Would she even want to see him after what he'd put her through? He took a deep breath of the cold night air. Callum had told him he had to grovel. Gemma had said the same thing. She'd insisted on looking after Joe so Morgan could go and do just that. So here he was, and for the first time in his life he felt unsure.

Suddenly the door swung open and Rebecca stood there, haloed by the Victorian pendant lamp that hung behind her.

"Morgan."

He dropped his hand, feeling foolish. "I was going to knock."

"Yes, I imagined that was what you were about to do. I was watching you from down the hall. But you took too long."

"Yeah, well, I wasn't sure whether you'd want to see me."

"I can see why you'd think that. What with you telling

me to trust you, right before I found out you were married—"

"*Was* married—"

"and have a child," she continued as if he hadn't spoken. "And that you're also going to leave. Yeah, I can imagine you'd think I wouldn't want to see you."

"Do you want to see me?"

She shrugged and opened the door. "Not particularly. But as you're here, you may as well come in. It's too cold to stand outside with one hand raised all night."

Morgan grunted, nodded his head and followed Rebecca inside, closing the door on the chill night. He went into the kitchen where she was filling the kettle. "Tea?"

He hated tea. "Great, thanks."

"Take a seat, it won't be long."

He sat on the small chintz-covered sofa and looked around and felt the ache in his heart tighten a little. The house was so like Rebecca. Pretty and sweet. But there was something more than that. It was homey. She'd created the home she'd always wanted. The home that meant so much to her. The home he could never ask her to leave.

"How's Joe?" She slid a mug of coffee over to him. "I know you don't like tea."

He nodded and took a sip. "He's good. Gemma's with him."

"She told you to come here?"

He nodded. There didn't seem to be any point in doing anything else.

"Hm. Thought she might. So what else did she tell you to do?"

"Grovel."

"Good advice. So go on then." She sat back and folded her arms expectantly.

"I'm sorry, Rebecca. I should have told you sooner."

"Damn right."

She still had her arms folded and her head was cocked to one side as if waiting for him to say something further. What else did he have to say to make things right? He cleared his throat. "It's just that I never talk to anyone about my personal life."

"Not even people *in* your personal life?"

"It's not happened before. Not like this."

She still looked unmoved. "Go on."

He licked his lips that suddenly felt dry. He hated talking about *anything*, let alone feelings. But he had to say the right thing now or else he might never have another chance. "You're not like other girls, you're different—" He stopped as soon as he'd said the word because he could see from her face that it was the wrong word.

"Different," she enunciated clearly. "How so? Strange—because I'm a scientist? Gauche—because I say what I think, even if those thoughts are a little... how would you say it, different?"

"You're twisting my words. I'm just trying to say that you're not like all the other girls"—he held up his hand when he saw her open her mouth to speak—"in a *good* way. I couldn't take my eyes off you from the first moment I saw you. And every time I saw you, I noticed something more about you." For the first time he could see her defenses drop and a warm light spark in her eyes. He was on the right track. "It was like, like..." He panicked for a moment as words failed him and then he had a brain wave. "It was like Gemma's painting of you. I watched her sketch in the lines first. And it was these lines that first drew me to you. And then she began painting in the different parts of you. How you held yourself, the tilt of your chin." Her arms unfolded and her lips curled into a soft smile. He sighed. "And your eyes, Rebecca." He couldn't help himself. He reached out and swept her cheek in a brief caress. She leaned into it and he kept his hand there. "Your eyes were the last part of you to be painted and they completed the picture. And then I knew."

"What?" she whispered.

"That I felt more for you than I'd ever done for anyone else. That I wanted you to be mine but that I could never ask you. *Never*. You were too good for me."

She turned her face into his hand and kissed the palm. He felt her touch all over his body. Then her lovely mouth turned up into a smile. "*That*, Morgan West, was a good grovel."

He grinned back. "It was harder than I thought."

Then her smile faded and she sat back in her chair and refolded her arms. His heart sank. "And what are your plans? Do you still intend to leave as soon as you can?"

"I can't."

"Can't?"

"No. Because that would mean leaving behind something too important to me."

She bit her lip. "Your job?"

"No." He rose and went over to her, extending his hand to hers. She took it and he pulled her to standing. He thrust his fingers through her hair and held her head steady, tilting it so it was closer to his. The time for groveling was over. It was time to take control again. "No," he repeated. "You." He dipped his head down to hers and kissed her.

By the time the kiss ended, Rebecca was trembling in his arms, her body pressed against his with a desire that matched his. Breathlessly she stepped away. For a moment he thought she'd regretted the kiss. But then a slow smile settled on her lips and she reached out and slipped a finger through a loop of his jeans.

"I want you, cowboy." Her eyes dropped and then raised to his with a smug look. "And I can see it's reciprocated. So what are we waiting for?"

"Do you trust me, Rebecca? I need to know."

She nodded. "I do. I feel I can be as wild as I like and I know you'll contain it, you'll hold me, you'll keep me safe."

"And I'll also enjoy it," he said, with a grin as he grabbed her hand and pulled her into the bedroom.

After they'd made love, Rebecca lay looking at the ceiling as her heart rate returned to normal. After a few seconds, Morgan got up and pulled on his trousers. He looked at her awkwardly as he did up his belt. "I have to go."

She allowed her gaze to roam over his glorious body, so strong and hard and yet which hid such a warm and loving heart. A heart that was leaving her. But only for now.

A huge lump appeared from nowhere and lodged in her throat. For the first time ever she didn't trust herself to speak. They'd made love before and she knew, without a doubt, they'd make love again. But something had changed between them; something had deepened and had become more intimate.

"Can't you stay a little longer?"

He shook his head. "I can't, Rebecca. You know I can't."

And she did. She pressed her lips together and rose, pulling on her dressing gown. "Yes, of course. I don't know why I asked." She flashed him a brief smile and walked over to the dressing table, picked up a hair tie and pulled her hair into a high ponytail. Behind her she could hear Morgan moving about the room, gathering his things. For a big man he moved quietly. She took a deep breath and turned to him. She'd hoped she'd collected herself sufficiently so he wouldn't be able to see how much she wanted him to stay. She never felt insecure, but now she did. She'd hoped her feelings of insecurity wouldn't be betrayed by the awkwardness of her movements. But she'd hoped in vain. Morgan stood silently watching her.

With one long stride he had her in his arms. "Look at me, Rebecca." He tilted her chin so she had no choice. "I want you in my life and we'll make time to be together. Here, at Glencoe, or in Shelter Springs, or wherever. But I have to make sure Joe is okay. He's been through a lot."

"Of course. Joe must be your priority. I'll fit in around him. There's no problem." She smiled reassuringly as she touched his cheek. "I don't want to pull you in different ways. *I* want what's best for Joe too. He's your son and so I... love him."

She bit her lip. She'd practically told Morgan that she loved him. It was the truth but she didn't think it was a truth he was ready to hear. She held her breath waiting to see what Morgan's response was. It wasn't what she'd hoped. He stepped away from her, as if in shock. "Right. Look, I have to go now. Thanks... for everything."

She grunted. "You don't have to thank me for sex."

"You know that's not what I mean. Thank you for understanding." He sighed. "Thank you for not making me grovel too hard." He grinned.

"I was going to but you're obviously not very good at it. I thought I'd better help you out."

"I'm grateful." He pulled her into his arms and she wanted him all over again.

"Um, and so am I..." she whispered. "Now go, before I drag you into bed again."

Rebecca followed Morgan into the hall, watched him walk out the door, down the small paved pathway, through the picket fence and into his ute. She stayed in the open doorway as the tail lights of his ute disappear down the street. She closed the door and leaned against it. He'd meant it when he'd apologized. He'd meant every word of it. He'd made love to her as if she truly were a princess—adoring every part of her. So why did she still feel uneasy?

"Joe worries me." Morgan accepted the beer from Callum and nodded to where Joe was playing with Dallas's older daughter, Lily, in the snow. "He hardly speaks to adults and if there's any sudden movement he looks terrified. And his nightmares..."

Callum walked up beside him and watched as Lily marched by followed by a distant-looking Joe. "Looks like he's having fun with Lily, though."

"I reckon Lily's the only person he ever talks to. I thought he'd be more settled by now."

"It's only been a few weeks. Give him time." Callum laughed. "Geez, look at Lily." Morgan followed his gaze to where Lily stood, bright eyed, having just sent a snowball flying at Joe. Hands on hips, she was taunting Joe over something. "That little girl of Dallas's is a monkey." He opened the window so they could hear what was being said.

"Boys don't throw things at girls," Joe replied to the unknown taunt. And he turned around and stomped off, leaving an indignant Lily running after him, tugging on his arm.

"Come on up to the tree-house and play," she urged.

Callum leaned out the window. "Not the tree-house, Lily, it's dangerous. Too icy."

"Okay!" she replied brightly at Callum, before running after Joe who'd stomped off to the cow barn.

"He loves his animals."

"He'll make a good farmer one day."

"Maybe." Morgan couldn't imagine that far ahead. With every day that passed since they'd arrived back in New Zealand, he'd come to realize that Leah had been right. Something *was* troubling Joe deeply and Morgan hadn't a clue what the problem was. The boy was too withdrawn, particularly with adults. Despite the incident with the snowball, Lily seemed to be the only person Joe really connected with.

He hated the feelings of frustration that swamped him when he couldn't fix a problem with a combination of number 8 wire and brute force. He looked out at the frozen lake which was framed with white, snow-laden trees out of one of which, a tree-house jutted darkly.

"The lake's frozen over just in time."

"Just in time for what?" Morgan asked distractedly.

"You were in Christchurch this time last year, weren't you? In time for the skating party at the weekend. All our friends and neighbors come." Callum looked at the tree-house, closed the window, and shook his head. "I must get that tree-house fenced off. Lily's my niece, I love her, but you better make sure she doesn't lead Joe into mischief. Like up that tree-house while it's so icy."

"Joe might not talk much but he's pretty obstinate. He'll only be led where he wants to go. Besides she hasn't persuaded him yet to go up the ladder to the tree-house. I can't see she'll get him up there in the ice."

Callum glanced up the massive oak to the high-up platform, complete with roof and window. "James made it, you know."

"James?"

"I know, it's hard to believe but he did."

"Hm! Didn't have him down for a carpenter."

"Used to love all that hands-on stuff. But then he grew up and discovered girls."

Morgan really didn't want to think about James and his girlfriends. He took a swig of beer and looked up at the sky, now leaden and dark. "Reckon it's going to snow later. Just as well we got those stragglers down from the high country today."

"Yeah, hell of a job. Thanks for that. You and the guys did well. I'd have been with you if it weren't for all this family business going on."

"You've the meeting with the lawyer tomorrow?"

"Yeah. Then it'll be over, thank God."

Morgan took another swig from his beer, thinking about the papers he'd had prepared for Callum a couple of days ago. They were upstairs in the room he was sharing with Joe, waiting until he'd found the right moment. Looks like that moment had come.

"You got a minute later? I'd like to show you something."

"Sure. What's it about—"

But before Morgan could reply Dallas and James walked into the room.

"Hey, you've started without us!" James exclaimed.

"Beer, not wine," Callum replied.

James shook his head and opened the door to the wine cellar. "You can keep your beer. I'll get us a good pinot noir." And he disappeared down the stone steps.

"How's it going, Morgan?" asked Dallas as he fixed

himself a soda water. Like his father before him, Dallas was an alcoholic but hadn't had a drink in nearly a decade. Unlike his father, he kept his ruthless streak only for the money markets.

Morgan turned to watch Joe come out of the cow shed hand in hand with Lily. "Joe's taking longer to settle in than I'd thought, although Lily's helping."

Dallas laughed. "Lily adores Joe. He's all she talks about."

It was Callum's turn to laugh. "You're going to have your hands full with Lily when she grows up."

Dallas rolled his eyes and sat down at the table. "Don't I know it. If I have my way I'll lock her in a nunnery during her teenage years. But Cassandra reckons she'll be fine. Wellington's a small city without the problems of bigger cities."

"Yes, the smaller the place, the easier it'll be to watch over them. Why do you think I'm staying at Glencoe?"

"Because, as from tomorrow you'll be the sole proprietor?"

"That, and because I can keep a very close eye on my kids growing up." Callum turned to Morgan. "I'm trying to persuade Morgan that he and Joe should stay."

Dallas looked at Morgan shrewdly. "It's a good place to grow up in."

"It might be if you've family around."

"Don't let Gemma hear you saying we're not your family."

Callum couldn't have said anything more guaranteed to shut Morgan up. But Callum didn't notice anything amiss as James re-entered the room. And when James entered a room, all eyes went to him. Morgan sat back and wondered again how someone could be so handsome and so charming, with so little effort.

"Mmm," James poured himself a glass of wine and sniffed it appreciatively. "Sorry I couldn't help with the mustering. Business and all that."

Callum rolled his eyes at Morgan. "Sure, little bro. Either business or a woman."

A few months ago and Morgan would have felt edgy in James's company but now he remembered Rebecca's reassurance. She hadn't been impressed with James and he no longer felt the invasive flicker of jealousy in James's company.

"Just business. While I'm here anyway. All the good ones have gone," he shot a wry look at Morgan.

"They've got sense," said Morgan grinning. He'd gotten used to the brothers now and enjoyed ribbing them, just as Callum did. Except this time James didn't look so happy. He gave a brief grin, finished his wine and stood up and replenished his glass.

"Anyhow, I'm off to the States next week. To Napa Valley. I've something big coming up I need to prepare for."

"Sounds mysterious," Dallas narrowed his eyes on his handsome younger brother. Is something going on I don't know about?"

"There's always something going on with James which neither of us know about. And I'm grateful we don't," said Callum.

"You've got your world, Callum, and I've got mine," James replied. "And, after tonight, once we've finally settled the division of assets between us, we'll all own our own business interests."

"Not that it'll make any practical difference," added Dallas.

"No," James replied. "But it's good to get it settled. I'm happy with the wineries, Dallas has his business interests and Callum has the land."

Callum grinned at Morgan. "Just as well my brothers don't have any interest in the land, otherwise I'd have a fight on my hands. Because there's no way I'm sharing Glencoe with anyone."

"And after that last fight we had as teenagers," Dallas raised his finger, from which a piece was missing, "I'm glad I don't have to fight you for the land."

"I'm kidding," said Callum. "Blood's thicker than water. I love the land, but family comes first. They always have and always will."

Suddenly Morgan had had enough and he scraped his chair back on the tiled floor with more force than he intended, and all three brothers suddenly looked up at him. He rose as casually as he could and rinsed out the beer bottle and placed it in the recycling bin.

"You might be like Callum in your love for the land, but you're better house-trained than he is," remarked James.

"It's not my house," said Morgan more evenly than he felt. "I'll go and get Joe, spend an hour with him and then catch up with you later, Callum. Around six?"

"Sure. I'll meet you in Mother's drawing room. It'll be quieter there."

"Bye, Dad!" And with that Joe had bolted out the door, down to where Gemma, Cassandra, Lily and Cassandra's youngest, Daniella, were waiting for him to watch the latest Disney film Gemma had organized. It was as if Joe couldn't wait to leave. And who could blame him? Morgan would have been the same, faced with a load of old photographs of people he didn't know.

Morgan had no idea why he'd shown the photographs to Joe. Desperation? A need for Joe to connect with his family? Whatever. They'd held no interest to a five-year-old.

Morgan picked up a photo of his mother, her head close to a handsome man, and held it up to the light of the small lamp beside Joe's bed. She'd been pretty, his mum. He sighed and placed the rest of the photos back into the shoe box, except for one which he continued to study, trying to find signs of likeness between him and his birth father. He didn't need to look far. It was pretty obvious.

Then he slipped it in his wallet and looked out the window. The snow on the mountains glowed with a ghostly light in the dusk of late winter and a sliver of moon sat alongside Venus. His mind immediately drifted back to Rebecca.

He glanced back at the papers in front of him and smoothed them down carefully. Had he made the right decision?

He turned each page over carefully after having read it for the tenth time, and then slowly read through the next page. Only when he'd reached the end did he sit back, tap the papers into an orderly pile, and look out of the small window that looked west, out to where the sun had already disappeared beyond the mountains, out to the land that he'd taken Rebecca to all those months ago.

He still didn't believe he was good enough for Rebecca but it didn't stop him thinking about her all the time, it didn't stop him craving her as soon as he'd left her. And the craving only intensified. He had to move things forward, get them all together under one roof and this was the best way he could think of.

His follow-up visit to the lawyer's a few days ago had shown him that his dream was attainable. Given Callum's willingness, that is.

The small chiming clock on the mantelpiece under which a small fire flickered in the hearth, struck six.

Morgan rose, sighed and picked up the papers. It was now or never. He walked down the hallway toward the drawing room where he'd been with Rebecca a few weeks earlier. That had been the first time he'd been in the room and he'd hardly noticed anything beyond the large family portraits. Not with Rebecca there to look at.

But she wasn't here now and when he entered the room and turned on the light the first thing he noticed was the absence of Callum. He'd been told he was here. The next thing he noticed was a small group of photographs mounted on the wall.

It was the informal atmosphere of the people in the photographs that drew him. People with their arms around each other, laughing, outdoors, having fun. Even though the photographs must have been taken from around the 1980s, they had a glamor that made him think of an earlier time in the 20th century. He supposed that not a lot had changed over the decades in the Mackenzie country, particularly at the old runs or stations.

He recognized Lady Mackenzie instantly. Even though she couldn't have been more than thirty, she had the same reserved demeanor, albeit tempered by a becoming shyness which she must have lost somewhere along the way. He could see the attraction she must have held for Sir Hugh Mackenzie. She was dressed beautifully and was surrounded by a group of equally beautifully dressed young women. The men were grouped together, enjoying being watched by the women while the servants waited on them.

In the foreground a little boy toddled determinedly along. It was unmistakably Dallas. Probably before Callum had been born. That figured.

He knew which one was Sir Hugh, knew his face, the strong handsome lines, the tall, broad figure, he'd seen photos before. Long before. So it wasn't his looks which made Morgan's heart stop, it was the person Sir Hugh was looking at with a heated expression that sparked a flash of anger. While ostensibly, Sir Hugh was looking at Lady Mackenzie, just behind her was another woman, a maid, who was blushing prettily and looking up at Sir Hugh from under flirtatious lowered lids.

Morgan stepped closer and swept away a trace of dust that lay on the glass over her face. Not just pretty, but beautiful. With her big blue eyes, her curvaceous figure and her curly blond hair peeping out from under a maid's hat, she'd turn any man's eye and, by the way Sir Hugh Mackenzie was looking at her, she'd turned his. It was a wonder that Lady Mackenzie allowed the photograph to be displayed. Maybe she simply didn't notice anyone beneath her.

Morgan pulled out the photograph from his wallet and studied it closely. Here the two of them were in a private moment. It must have been taken at some photo booth in a small town nearby where the photographer wouldn't know them. Some weekend tryst no doubt, where Sir Hugh wouldn't be recognized.

Suddenly the door opened and Callum strolled in.

"Hey, Morgan."

He came up beside him, just as Morgan stuffed the old photo into the back of his jeans where his other papers were. "I was looking at these old family photos."

Callum looked up at them. "Pop used to enjoy all that stuff. That's Dallas there." He pointed to the front of the picture. "And that's Mother, doing what she does best, organizing everyone and hosting events." He turned back to Callum. "So what did you want to give to me?"

"These." Morgan pulled out the papers, and the photo fluttered onto the thick carpet.

Callum and Morgan locked eyes. Morgan couldn't move. "Who's this?" Callum frowned, picking up the photo, holding between his fingers. "It's Pop. Who's he with? I don't recognize her? A girlfriend before he married?" He tilted it to the light. "No, he's wearing his wedding ring." He looked back at Morgan. "Who the hell is this?"

Morgan closed his eyes briefly. He'd never wanted this. How could he have been so stupid?

"Morgan?" Callum shook his head in confusion. "What are you doing with this photograph of my father and some woman?"

"She's not *some* woman." He plucked the photograph from Callum's hands before Callum could stop him, and looked at it, looked at that beautiful face, so full of hope. "That woman is my mother."

"Your *mother*?"

"Yes."

"And what is she doing with my father in this photograph?"

"What do you think?" Despite Morgan's intention never to bring up the subject with Callum, he felt indignant at Callum's attitude.

"Your mother? My father?"

"Yes."

"They had an affair?"

"Yes. Mum grew up in Shelter Springs. I think the affair must have started before she got work at Glencoe. Made it easier, I guess, if she was a maid here."

Callum swore, raked his fingers through his hair and walked over to the other side of the room. "I knew my father had had affairs, but right under Mother's nose?" He shook his head and sighed heavily. "What a bastard."

"He was that all right."

Callum paced back to look at the photograph on the wall. "And she's here?"

Morgan pointed her out. "She loved working at Glencoe. It was all I heard about growing up. How they did things properly at the big house, what beautiful clothes Lady Mackenzie had, what wonderful food they had to eat. And always, what a true gentleman Sir Hugh Mackenzie was."

Callum snorted. "She couldn't have known him that well."

"She saw what she wanted to see."

Callum peered closer at the photograph. "I don't remember her growing up. So I hadn't been born then, but Dallas had."

"No. Lady Mackenzie gave her her marching orders shortly after that photograph was taken. Must have been about six months later, I reckon."

"Why?"

Callum had turned away from the photograph and was facing Morgan now. Morgan hesitated. But it was too late. He had to tell Callum the truth and let him make of it what he would. And, knowing Callum, as he'd come to know him, he didn't think he'd like what Morgan was about to tell him.

"It seems Lady Mackenzie didn't take kindly to a pregnant maid, particularly when she probably didn't trust her husband as far as she could throw him."

"Your mother was pregnant..." Callum trailed off. He simply stared at Morgan. Callum's face hardened as he understood the full import of Morgan's words. "You? *You* are my half-brother? Is that what you're trying to tell me?"

"I'm not *trying* to tell you anything. I'm telling you straight. Sir Hugh Mackenzie was my father. I'm your half-brother, like it or not."

CHAPTER TEN

Callum took a step closer and Morgan could see the depth of anger in his eyes. "And I *don't* like it, Morgan, not one bit."

"You're not the only one. I'm not best pleased either that your scumbag of a father was also mine."

Callum snorted as if he didn't believe Morgan. "So, do you have proof of this?"

"Proof?" Morgan faced Callum eye to eye. They were the same height except Morgan was a shade broader and stronger from a life of outside work. "Yeah, I've got proof. He wrote her a couple of letters which I'm sure he regretted. Paid her off too. We've got proof of that as well."

"Is his name on your birth certificate?"

"Yes. Anything else you need to know?"

"Yes." Callum remained close to Morgan. His icy anger would have been intimidating to anyone other than Morgan. "I want to know what it is you want."

Morgan shook his head. "Want? I've never wanted anything from you, or any of the Mackenzies."

"I don't believe you."

"Seems like you've made up your mind that I want something. Tell me, what do you think it is I've come here for?"

"Stop playing games, Morgan. It's obvious, isn't it? There can be no other reason you chose to come back over a year ago when the news broke about the settlement of the Mackenzie estate. I guess its delay was the only reason you stayed on. You want a share, don't you?"

Morgan snorted. "Well, if that's what you think, I guess you're right." He suddenly remembered the papers in his pocket and saw how it would now look to Callum. Despite the fact that Morgan realized Callum's suspicions were entirely reasonable given the circumstances, Morgan was infuriated. Let Callum—let them all—think what the hell they liked. What did it matter what any of them thought about him?

"So when were you going to share this information? Had something a bit more dramatic planned?"

"Do you think I was going to rush into the lawyers, just as you were signing the final documents, and wave my birth certificate around?"

"You tell me."

Callum's face was hard and angry. Morgan could see there would be no getting through to him. And at that moment, he couldn't have cared less. The papers in his pocket were nothing to what he could claim. He paused and for one long moment considered being the man Callum imagined him to be and claiming everything he could. But that man wasn't him. There was no way he'd mess up this man's life, this man he'd called a friend up to a short time ago. He might never be a friend again but Morgan could never take from Callum what he valued most.

"You tell me," Callum repeated through gritted teeth.

Morgan bit back his anger. He wouldn't ruin Callum but he might let him stew a bit. "All three of you are meeting with the lawyers tomorrow, right?"

Callum nodded, barely able to contain his anger.

"Then I'll see you there."

"You bastard," Callum muttered.

"Correct. And whose fault was that? Not mine, *not* my mother's, but *our* father's. And he owes me. Have you any idea what it was like growing up with a father who refused to have anything to do with me?"

"And you think that entitles you?"

"I don't *think*, I *know*." With each passing comment of Callum's, Morgan grew more and more angry, dredging years of bitterness to the surface. "Remember, Callum, I'm older than you. Your brothers might not be interested in Glencoe, but farming's in my blood." Morgan turned away and walked to the door.

"Get out of my house!" Callum called after him.

Morgan stopped and turned slowly, fury pulsing through his veins. Fury against the Mackenzies and how they treated his mother all those years ago. "I'll leave when I'm good and ready."

"Of course. You've moved into the homestead. It was all part of your plan, wasn't it? All along, you've been maneuvering yourself to be in this position. How could I have been sucked in so easily?"

Morgan paused, white hot anger filling his veins. "I don't know. Perhaps you're weaker, more like our father, than you thought."

Morgan closed the door behind him and went to his bedroom, the room he shared with Joe. His son. The only member of his family who mattered now.

It was the knock at her front door which awoke her. Rebecca blinked slowly and glanced at the clock. It was midday. Everyone knew she didn't get in from night work until seven in the morning. Everyone knew she was a no-go area until at least two in the afternoon. Particularly Morgan, whose knock it was. No one else knocked like that, she thought. One knock—loud enough for her to hear wherever she was in the small cottage. Typical of him. He only had to do something once to make a point. Still, knowing it was him at the door, all feelings of tiredness disappeared as her body responded at the thought of him.

Her heat leaped. She'd only seen him the previous night, before she left for work but she rushed to the door, tying her robe as she went, eager to see him again. She opened the door wide. "Morgan." She stepped toward him and then stopped abruptly as she looked down into Joe's pensive face.

Morgan's hands lightly kneaded the little boy's shoulders, protectively, reassuringly. The little boy's eyes were large and anxious, as usual. It made her heart melt to see his insecurity.

She dropped her hand to her side, pulling her robe more tightly around her. She swept her hair from her face. "Joe! How lovely to see you. Come in."

She stood to one side to let them in. "An unexpected pleasure, Morgan."

He nodded grimly and walked past her into the kitchen, where bright sunshine streamed in, reflecting off the yellow painted walls and the polished wood of the table and bookcases. Rebecca didn't try to hug Joe, or touch him, as she knew from experience that it made Joe feel uncomfortable.

"Joe?" prompted Morgan.

"Hello, Rebecca," Joe dutifully said.

"Hi. Fancy a hot chocolate? With froth on?"

"Yes please."

"Why don't you go and play with the toys and the train set in the front room while I get us all some drinks?" She could see Morgan had something on his mind and the toy box was also out of earshot. Joe should have been at school in Shelter Springs at this time of day and Morgan was always busy somewhere on Glencoe. "I'll put on a CD you might like." She flicked on the music and then returned to Morgan.

They both watched Joe quietly sit down and begin playing with the train set Rebecca had set up for him alongside a bookcase full of her old favorites.

Rebecca stepped into the kitchen and Morgan followed her. She'd hardly had time to turn before he pulled her to him and gave her a big hug. She stepped back and looked up at him, her arms snaking around his neck. "What's up?"

The muscles flickered in his jaw and his eyes were red with exhaustion. "It's all a mess." He pulled away from her and walked over to the kitchen sink, gripped it and looked out the window. "All a bloody mess."

She walked up behind him and hesitated, feeling the tension coming off him in waves. "Tell me. Is it Joe? His mother?"

"No." They glanced through the serving hatch at Joe who was playing, unable to hear their words. "No, Joe's... the same."

"Then, what? I don't understand."

He turned in her arms, pushing back her hair, looking everywhere except her eyes. She reached up and held his face firm between her two hands. "Look at me, Morgan.

And tell me what's wrong. You're scaring me. Is anything the matter with you? Are you ill?"

He looked down at her then. "No, I'm not ill. I'm sorry, Rebecca. After all I've said... But I've no choice. I've come to tell you we won't be here after tonight. We'll be gone this time tomorrow. Me and Joe. We can't stay."

She froze. She literally froze. It was as if the blood had drained from her, leaving her without warmth—chill and numb.

She opened her mouth to speak but no words had formed, and her mouth was suddenly dry as fear gripped her.

"Rebecca?" He took her hands from his head and put them into his own, cradling them. "Say something."

She shook her head. "You're... What? You're leaving?"

He nodded, the line between his eyebrows, furrowing further with concern.

"But, why? Didn't you mean what you said before? All that stuff about staying to be here for Joe and me. What was that all about?"

"Of *course* I meant it. I'd made plans, plans that could have given us a future. But not now..."

"Tell me. I don't understand." She tried to keep her voice even, to stop it from shaking but a sob came up from nowhere and broke up the last word.

"I had to tell Callum the truth about me."

Confusion broke through the paralysis of fear. "The truth about you? Don't *I* know the truth about you? What are you talking about?"

"It was never my intention—you have to believe me—to tell him. I came here just to see... just to stay a season and then go. But then I met you."

"You're not making any sense."

He exhaled roughly. "No, I'm not. Because none of this does." He took her hands again and looked into her eyes. "Callum is my half-brother. My mother and Hugh Mackenzie had an affair. She was forced to leave, paid off by him and we both conveniently disappeared."

Her eyes widened with each word uttered. "You. And Callum. Are brothers?"

"Half-brothers."

She blinked, relieved. "Wow! I always thought you looked alike." She shook her head, half-laughing. "That's amazing. I mean, it's awful what happened to your mum, but that you've found your half-brother and that you both really like each other, that bit's really great."

"No, it's not. Callum and I had an argument. He's not happy about the situation and nor am I. I have no option but to leave."

"No! Surely there's a way out of this. He's a rational man and you're, well, sort of rational."

"Thanks very much."

"Surely you can resolve whatever the issues are." She hesitated as her logical mind quickly assessed what the issues might be. "Is Callum upset by what his father's done? About his father's affair? Worried about what his mother might say when she finds out?"

"I don't think that worried him. From what Callum has said in the past, I don't think anything would surprise him about his father."

"Is it because he's been taken by surprise? Maybe you just need to give him time to get used to the idea. After all it's been kind of dumped on him while you've lived with this all your life."

"Yeah. I've had my whole life knowing I'm a bastard.

Reckon I don't feel that sorry for Callum. He's had everything handed to him on a plate."

"I don't know about that. From what Gemma says his
father was pretty mean to all of them."

"He got it easy, believe me."

She shook her head. "Why did you come here, Morgan?
You must have known what it would be like."

He shrugged. "I saw a piece in the paper about Glencoe
formally changing hands. I hadn't thought much of the
place up till then. So I thought why not go and see if it was
like Mum had described."

"And was it?"

"Pretty much. Even though life here was good, I knew
I'd never fit in. One season and then I'd move on, that's
what I thought. Keep moving, just as I've always done since
Leah and Joe left. Then I met you. And I thought I'd stay a
little longer. But you were always too good for me."

"Why would you say such a thing?"

"Come on. Think of that list of yours. I'll bet I'm not
even close to matching up to it."

A lump rose into her throat from nowhere. She blinked.
"Weren't you?"

"Not unless you changed each point on it to the opposite, no."

She tried to smile, thinking of all the changes she'd
made to her list since she'd met Morgan. "True. But why
move now?" She tried to shrug, tried to keep things cool.

"Callum believes I'm after a share in the property."

"He believes what? But that's ridiculous. How on earth
did he get that idea?"

"Because that's what I led him to believe."

The microwave beeped and Rebecca jumped. Mind
racing, she pulled away from Morgan and focused on

making Joe his hot chocolate, thankful for the opportunity to process this piece of totally illogical information.

She stirred in the chocolate and reached into the cupboard for a marshmallow, selected a couple of white ones—she'd sussed out pretty quickly that Joe didn't like pink—and dropped one onto the chocolate and the other on the saucer. Just the thought of little Joe moving on brought tears to her eyes. She bit her lip and plucked another couple of marshmallows out of the bag and placed them on the saucer.

She took the drink over to Joe. "Here you go, Joe." She could hear the false note of cheer in her voice and by the alert expression on Joe's face, he'd noticed it too. You couldn't fool kids. "I'll put it on the coffee table. It's still a bit hot."

Her mind raced, trying to figure out if she'd got Morgan wrong all these months, as she watched Joe take a sip of froth before rolling onto his stomach again to carefully push a train into a siding. She continued to watch, not wanting to look at Morgan with a face full of uncertainty, as Joe assembled the little train figures—the engineer, the controller—around the train with great precision. He sat back on his haunches and got another train and with full force bashed it into the first train, sending the little figures flying everywhere. Then he got another little figure from the second train and began making shooting noises.

"What are you doing, Joe?" Morgan asked. Rebecca hadn't heard him come into the room.

Joe stopped playing and his actions became careful once more. "Just playing."

"Looks like there's been a bit of a crash." Morgan dropped down to his son's level and picked up the man who was killing everyone. "And who's this guy?"

"He's the mean guy who kills people."

"Why's he killing people?"

"Because he wants their money. That's what mean guys do."

"Not that often."

Joe turned his little face up to Morgan. "They do if they want money for drugs. I've seen it." The atmosphere changed immediately and Joe felt it. A shadow fell over his face and he turned away. "I have." He stuck out his bottom lip mutinously.

"Where did you see it?"

"At home."

"In LA?"

"Yeah. Not LA like on telly, LA. But where Mum and me and Mum's friends lived."

Morgan closed his eyes briefly as if he were in pain and then he looked over to Rebecca who had trouble holding back the tears. Playing with the train set had opened Joe up in a way that talking hadn't. The kid was scared of the world because his old world had terrified him. And no wonder.

Morgan knelt down beside him. "Maybe we should get the good guys some help?" He rummaged in the toy box and found a helicopter. "Maybe the good guys can swoop in and make everything okay. Hey?"

Joe shrugged. "Maybe."

"Let's try."

Rebecca returned to the kitchen and made Morgan and her hot drinks, watching them play together through the hatch. Any doubts she had that Morgan might undermine Callum's claim to Glencoe evaporated in just that one act. She had Morgan pegged all right. He was a kind, honorable man who'd rather die, rather inflict injury on himself, than hurt the people he loved and respected. He'd get Joe through this. And he'd make no claim on the Glencoe lands, no demands on Callum. But who was there to look out for him?

Rebecca reached for her phone and sent a text to Gemma.

"Each is as dumb as the other." Gemma sat back in her chair in the café, her eyes bright with anger. "My grandpa used to say he'd box my ears if I didn't stop being a pain and that's what they need—their ears boxing. They're acting like little kids."

"I think your parenting skills need brushing up," smiled Rebecca.

"You know what I mean."

Rebecca rolled her eyes. "I know *just* what you mean. I can't understand why Callum would believe Morgan would do a thing like that. Morgan hasn't an acquisitive bone in his body. He doesn't demand anything from anyone."

"Callum knows that really. I think he's just scared. Glencoe means everything to him and he's never had a moment's doubt, growing up, that it would always be his to run as he wanted. Dallas and James have other interests and were more than happy to let Callum manage the lot." Gemma paused. "And the timing thing. That Morgan should show up just at the moment that everything was to be ratified." She shook her head. "It's a real coincidence."

"No, it's not."

"What do you mean?"

"Morgan told me that he saw something in the paper about Glencoe almost two years ago which got him thinking. And that something was related to the final wind up of the estate. The finalization of the estate wasn't why he's here, but the media surrounding it highlighted it."

"Ah, that makes sense. And I'm sure it'll make sense to Callum." Gemma sighed. "He knows. I'm sure he knows. But these guys are just so damned stubborn. Once they've made a stand, it's hell getting them to back down. Any ideas?"

Rebecca sat forward in her chair. "Funny you should ask."

Half an hour later they both left the café with smug grins on their faces.

Three pairs of hard eyes met Morgan as he entered the Mackenzie family's lawyer's office.

James was sitting down, one ankle hooked over his leg. He shook his head in disbelief and brushed a piece of imaginary fluff off his suit trousers.

Dallas stood behind the lawyer, looking over some papers and Callum stood with his back against the wall, as if he'd just turned from looking out the window.

The lawyer rose and extended his hand. "Mr..."

"West. Morgan West."

"Please, be seated."

"No thanks, mate. I'd rather stand. This won't take long."

"You reckon?" scowled Callum.

"Yeah, I reckon."

"Well." The lawyer looked over his glasses anxiously at the others. "If you're ready, then maybe we should begin."

Dallas came and stood, arms folded, between Callum and Morgan. James was the only brother who was seated.

"Sure," said James, "I think we'd all appreciate this being wound up as soon as possible."

Morgan had never felt so uncomfortable in all his life. But he'd come to a decision. For Rebecca and for Joe, he'd stand his ground and press ahead with his original plans. So he remained standing alongside Dallas and Callum as the lawyer droned through some preliminaries. Then he stopped and looked up at Morgan with a little trepidation.

"And, I understand Mr. West that you wish to make a claim."

"A claim?"

"That you're the... illegitimate son of Sir Hugh Mackenzie. And"—he peered at the three brothers—"I have to say that the information appears correct."

"Yes, that's right. I am."

Callum turned to face him squarely and Morgan turned towards him, ignoring Dallas who stood in the way, and the lawyer whose voice couldn't be heard above the Mackenzie brother's deep voices.

"So what do you intend to do about it, then?" asked Callum.

"I've come to make you an offer."

Callum scoffed. "Right. How much of my inheritance do you want?"

Morgan handed him the papers he'd intended to show Callum a few days ago. "The land that borders Shelter Lake. It's not much use to you. Too far away from a good road to move sheep along, and too far away from good shelter. But if you lease it to me I can make it productive."

Callum raised his eyebrows and took the papers. "That's all you want? And you want to lease it?"

"Yeah. Look at the papers. I don't want anything for nothing. The price I'm willing to pay is there."

Callum pressed his lips together as he read and then looked up at Morgan. "Where are you getting this money?"

"I've not stolen it, if that's what you're thinking. It's all above board. Your father paid my mother off years ago to keep her quiet. And she was. She invested the money for me but I never touched it. I never wanted anything to do with it, but I've sold the investments now that I've Joe to consider. Take it or leave it."

"Is that it?" asked Dallas frowning as he looked from Callum to Morgan. "You're not making any other claim on the land."

"It's not my land to claim." Morgan didn't take his eyes off Callum. "I think your brother jumped to the wrong conclusion."

James shook his head and looked at all three of them. "All this drama for nothing? Well, Callum? It's your land. What do you think?"

"I think... it's a good proposal. I haven't found the right use for the land till now. This should work." He narrowed his gaze thoughtfully onto Morgan. "Is this for Joe?"

Morgan nodded. "And for Rebecca. And for me."

James extended his hand to Morgan. "Looks like you've got yourself a deal, Morgan. Congratulations." He turned to the lawyer. "Now, if that's all agreed, perhaps we could move on with the rest of the business."

Callum stepped forward and dropped the papers on the desk and scrawled his name at the bottom. Morgan counter-signed and stepped away. "I'll leave you to it."

"Thank you, Mr. West. I'll have the paperwork finalized and my office will be in touch."

Morgan nodded and without looking at any of the brothers walked out the door. He'd done what he'd come to do. He didn't expect them to like it and he didn't expect their friendship to survive it.

As he stepped out onto the cold Shelter Springs street he glanced up at the land he'd shown Rebecca all those weeks ago, the land that was now his to farm, his to build a house on, his to begin a new life with Joe... and maybe, if she'd have him, Rebecca too. But he didn't feel the thrill of ownership that he'd expected. He glanced back at the office where the shape of Callum could still be seen by the window. No, he felt only disappointment.

With the deed done, Gemma and Rebecca sneaked back into the homestead, giggling like two school kids.

"I've never done anything this naughty before," said Rebecca sitting down, stunned at what she'd just done.

"Becks, I've done so many things that are wrong, that I know when something is right or not." She poured them both coffees and brought Rebecca's over to her. "And this is right, believe me."

"I do." Rebecca sipped the coffee. "Or at least I think I do."

The sound of cars approaching made Gemma jump up from the table and look out the window. "Looks like we made it just in time. The guys are back."

Rebecca followed Gemma's gaze as Dallas, Callum, and James got out of the car. Dallas and James came straight up the steps into the house while Callum walked purposefully across the paddock toward the barn.

Rebecca and Gemma looked at each other in alarm. "The barn! You said Callum wouldn't go there."

Gemma grabbed her coat. "There's nothing there for

him to do. He must be wanting some time on his own. I'll go and stop him."

As Gemma left through the back door, the other door opened and James and Dallas stepped inside.

"Rebecca! What a lovely surprise." James kissed her on both cheeks while she blushed furiously.

Dallas poured a coffee and sat down at the table, looking at her intently. "We've just been in a meeting with Morgan."

"Oh," breathed Rebecca, wishing she were anywhere but here. She took another sip of her coffee but when she raised her eyes, Dallas was still looking at her.

"So when's the happy occasion?"

She frowned. "What happy occasion?"

Dallas snorted. "Don't tell me he's not popped the question yet? He's as bad as Callum—doing things back to front." He shook his head. "I don't know why we didn't see the similarity between them before."

Rebecca took her coffee cup to the sink and rinsed it out before stacking it into the dishwasher, trying to figure out what Dallas was talking about and how to make her escape. This was getting way too complicated for her liking.

"Anyway, I hope you'll all be very happy together," Dallas continued.

"I'm sure they will," said James.

She took a deep breath and turned to face them. "Thank you." She smiled, wondering what else she could add when she didn't have the first idea what they were talking about. "I'm... sure we will." She shrugged on her coat and picked up her bag. "I'm off."

"See you later then?"

She turned, frowning, to James. "Why?"

"Don't tell me you've forgotten about the famous

Glencoe ice-skating party?" He nodded his head to all the activity around the frozen lake, where street vendor carts were being set up offering the traditional roasted chestnuts and the expected hot chips, as well as enough hot drinks to warm the insides of the coldest skater.

"Oh yes, *that*. Sure."

"I'll see you later, then. And Rebecca?"

She turned to James. "Yes?"

"Don't give Morgan too hard a time. He adores you, that's plain to see."

"Hm." She smiled a brief and non-committal smile, and went out the door. She didn't look behind her, or even glance at the activities around the lake. All she could think about was getting in the car and finding Morgan and giving him a very hard time. And not in a good way.

CHAPTER ELEVEN

Morgan drove into the Glencoe yard which had been set aside as a temporary car park. He'd been in town with Joe looking at alternative accommodation all afternoon. No way was he going to continue to stay at Glencoe. He wouldn't be here now if it weren't for the numerous text messages he'd received from Rebecca.

It had been Joe who'd discovered his phone, on silent, slipped down the side of a seat. And it had been Joe who'd carefully read out message after message from Rebecca saying she needed to see him urgently. The last message had been the clincher. Something about Joe being expected at the ice-skating party... some activity he'd been working on. The message had been vague and Joe had looked puzzled. But when he'd received another text message from Gemma along similar lines Morgan had decided to come. After all, it would give Joe a chance to say goodbye to everyone before they moved their things into a motel.

And it'd give him a chance to see Rebecca... to talk to Rebecca.

Morgan slammed the ute door behind Joe who'd immediately run off to join Lily. It made Morgan feel bad. The lad had settled into Glencoe these past few weeks and now he was going to take him away again. But what choice did he have? This place wasn't—and would never be—his home. He sighed and looked around Glencoe—at the trees, the land, the pale gold of the grass topped with the white sheen of frost which still held its grip on the cold land. Joe wasn't the only one who'd miss this place. Morgan began to make his way toward the lake.

There were people everywhere. The Mackenzies sure knew how to throw a party. Now the afternoon was fading into evening, the lights in the trees around the lake had been lit and twinkled like stars in the sky, reflecting on the ice of the lake, as children and adults alike swept around the ice, skimming along in fancy figures, while others staggered around the shoreline. Laughter and shrieks of delight filled the air.

He looked about for Rebecca but didn't see her. Instead of joining the others, he walked to a quiet corner of the property, where he could observe without being observed, where he could watch Joe and look out for Rebecca without having to mingle with the Mackenzie brothers.

He could see Joe from his vantage point. He hadn't been skating yet and was sitting to the side amongst his new friends drinking hot drinks from which steam billowed out into the cold air.

He should be down there with him, but he couldn't bring himself to face up to Callum and the rest of the family. His mother had been right. Glencoe was a beautiful place. But it was a place where he wasn't wanted and after all he'd been through he could do without being hated by the bloody Mackenzies.

He kicked the heel of his boot against the wall behind

him, venting the anger that simmered as he watched Lady Mackenzie greet the public as if she were royalty. And Callum—a man who he'd always thought of as more friend than boss—how could he have believed that Morgan would have taken the things he valued most?

And where was Rebecca? He pushed himself off the barn wall and began to walk away.

"Morgan!" He turned to see her striding toward him with a very determined look on her face. The setting sun shone on her dark hair that escaped the brightly colored beanie. "What's all this about you making plans about me, about my future without even telling me?" Her breath formed clouds in the increasingly frigid air. She stood in front of him with her hands on her hips.

"What? Who told you that?"

"It doesn't matter who told me. Is it true?"

"Yes, it's true. But—"

"So..." Her lips tightened and he knew he was in for a telling off. But the way her flushed cheeks and bright eyes reminded him of making love to her, made him think that being told off by her wouldn't be without its pleasures. "So you think you can be this big macho cowboy and go around making decisions not only about you and your son's future, but about mine too?"

He shrugged. "I guess." Her eyes looked almost violet in the changing light. He could look at them for hours. He only just managed preventing a smile of pleasure from settling on his lips.

"You *guess*, do you? And what gives you the authority to go around making life decisions for me?"

He shrugged again, desperately trying to refrain from pulling her to him, of feeling the warmth of her body against his and of burrowing his face into her hair and inhaling her. "I thought we could get married."

She stepped back, hands on hips. "Did you, indeed? And why exactly did you think we could do this? Don't tell me you have a list and I fit the criteria, because I won't believe you."

"No, I leave all that kind of stuff to you. I know I'm not your ideal man, Rebecca, but I reckon we could make a go of it."

"*Go of it?* Man, you could really do with some help in the charm department. Maybe I should arrange a meeting with you and James. He can charm the birds from the trees."

Any thought of her lovely eyes, the feel of her hair against his cheek disappeared in an instant. He didn't need to hide a smile any more. He folded his arms. "If you want charm, then perhaps you're right. Perhaps you *should* see him."

"Maybe I will." She turned on her heels and began to walk away.

"Before you go, you might answer my question."

She stopped suddenly and shouted over her shoulder. "I might have done, if you'd damn well asked me one!" And then she continued to walk away.

Women! Morgan whistled for Annie—the only female who seemed to understand him. He watched Rebecca walk up to a surprised James who instinctively flashed her a flirtatious smile. He pitied the woman who fell in love with him. He doubted if James knew the meaning of the word faithful.

He started to walk away from the party, out to the open fields, when he heard his name being called. He turned to see Gemma running up to him.

"Morgan! Glad I found you. Looks like some kids have got into the barn and loosened the hay bales. It's pretty dangerous apparently. If any more kids get in the lot could fall down on top of them. Would you mind dealing with it?"

He frowned, wondering why she'd asked him when there were other estate workers whose job it was. No doubt instructed by Callum, he thought bitterly.

"Sure."

He watched Gemma return to the party before walking quickly over to the barn which was some distance away. He scanned it. It looked fine to him. He briefly wondered how Gemma could have known about it. Maybe one of the kids alerted her. Then he took a closer look. Someone *had* tampered with it. It wouldn't have taken long but he wondered who'd done such deliberate damage. It would take hours to set right. But it was too dangerous to leave. It'd have to be done there and then.

In the time it took to collect his tools and begin work, the light from the open door darkened and Callum entered. "What the hell?" he said as he plucked away loose straw.

"Looks like kids," Morgan said without looking up.

Callum swore under his breath as he inspected the damage. "Everyone else is skating or drinking."

"Best give me a hand then." He tossed Callum a wire cutter. He caught it and came around and looked at what Morgan had done.

"Looks good. You just putting some more wire around it?"

"Yeah, giving it a bit of a tidy up at the same time. Should be fine."

Callum nodded and dropped to his haunches beside Morgan. "You do that, and I'll pull it tight behind."

They worked in silence for some time with only the

distant sound of the people on the lake, and the wind rustling in the leaves of the tall trees that had grown out of the original fence posts planted behind the barn.

"Do you think we'll get it fixed before dark?" Callum looked at the work they had still to do.

"Temporarily fixed at any rate."

Callum set to work beside Morgan. "Bloody kids."

At the end of an hour, Callum stood up and stretched, watching as Morgan finished. Morgan put the tools back in his bag and slung it over his shoulder. "That'll do for now."

Callum grunted and nodded as they both surveyed their handiwork. Then Callum turned to Morgan and held out his hand. "Thanks, mate. I'll get some men to fix it permanently tomorrow."

Morgan hesitated only a moment before he took it and they shook. "No problem."

Together they walked out into the now dark evening except for the lights around the homestead and the lake.

Morgan pulled down his hat and looked up into the sky in which stars were beginning to appear. "I don't want anything from you, you know. Just the leasehold, at commercial rates. That's all."

It was Callum's turn to hesitate. He didn't look at Morgan either. "Yeah, I know. Sorry, it's just…"

"Yeah, I know."

They shuffled a little on the icy ground. "We'd better get back to the party. They'll be wondering where we are."

They fell into step across the paddock. "You maybe," said Morgan.

"Oh, I can think of at least a couple of people who'd be wondering where you are."

It was Morgan's turn to grunt noncommittally.

"I told Mother."

"About me?"

"Yeah. She knew of course about Dad and... your mother. But had no idea you were the child."

"Don't tell me, she wants me gone."

"No. She wants to meet you. Properly, this time." They stopped at the rear entrance to the homestead. "Have you got a few minutes?"

"I guess." Morgan began to open the back door.

"No," Callum said. "Mother was clear that she wanted you to use the front door."

Morgan laughed and shook his head, remembering his first night at Glencoe when she'd turned him away.

"I know what you're thinking, but Mother's from a different generation. She's trying to apologize."

"Must be hard for her."

"It is."

They walked around the front of the house where Lady Mackenzie stood, framed by the light spilling out from the hallway. She was as beautifully dressed as ever. She extended her hand to his. "Morgan."

He reached out and shook hands. She stepped to one side. "Please come inside and have a cup of tea."

"I can't, Lady Mackenzie. Joe's outside. I've left him for long enough. But thank you."

She nodded and bit her lip. Morgan could see the effort it cost her, could see she was trying to do the right thing. "Of course. I just want you to know that I'm sorry for the way things worked out. For you and your mother. My husband, well he..."

"It's history, Lady Mackenzie. History. Forget it."

Then she looked at him with her piercing blue eyes that were full of sadness. "I don't forget anything. Least of all my husband's weaknesses, nor my mistakes. I shouldn't have dismissed her like I did. It wasn't right."

Morgan was shocked and by a quick glance at Callum, he could see he was equally astonished at his mother's admission. They were both speechless.

"I tried to make amends. I hope the money I sent her came in useful?"

Morgan's mouth fell open. "You? It was you who gave Mum all that money?"

"Yes, of course. I wanted to do the right thing... after I'd done the wrong thing, you see." She gave him a brief unhappy smile. "I hope it helped."

He nodded. There was no way he could tell Lady Mackenzie that his mother hadn't been able to access the funds while they'd been held virtual prisoners in the bush for so many years. He nodded again, focusing on the time when they'd returned to Hokitika. "Yes, Mum and I eventually settled in Hokitika and we invested your money. Thank you," he added as an afterthought.

"Good. She was a good woman. A lovely woman. She was my friend once. Before..."

His mother had never told him this bit. "She thought highly of you, too. I heard all about life at Glencoe and about you."

Her smile was warmer now as she remembered earlier times. Then she nodded sadly. "Thank you, Morgan. You go and join your son. I think I'll retire now." She looked up at Callum. "Callum? Would you make my excuses to our visitors?"

"Of course, mother. Are you feeling well?"

"Quite well, thank you. Quite well."

Callum and Morgan watched her walk across the wide

hallway, her head still held high but without her usual brisk gait.

Callum and Morgan walked outside and stood for a few moments looking down at the party. "I've never seen my mother like that before," Callum said in a wondering, low voice. "It's like she's a different person."

Morgan caught his eye. "I reckon we all do what we have to do in difficult times. Cover up what we're really like to hide the hurt. And she must have had a lot of hurt to hide because of Sir Hugh."

"Yeah, I guess you're right." Callum sighed and then glanced over at Rebecca and Gemma who had their heads together cooing over Violet. "You and Rebecca are serious then?" Callum continued.

"*I'm* serious about Rebecca. Not so sure she is about me."

"Don't think you've any problems there. Gemma says she's head over heels over you."

Morgan grunted. "I don't think I'm her type."

"Gemma's never wrong about these things. I don't know how women know this kind of stuff, but they do." Callum shrugged. "Can't fight it, mate."

They paused on the edge of the garden just as they were about to part ways. Callum to join his family and Morgan to hang around on the edges of the party, waiting for a convenient moment when he could talk to Rebecca.

"Thanks again for your work just now," Callum said. "Just as well you're still here. I'd never have finished that on my own before dark."

"Sure you would."

"Fancy a drink with me and the family?"

"Thanks, but no. I'm only here because Joe made something or other for the kid's display. Rebecca insisted I didn't leave until after that."

"Kid's display?" Callum frowned. "What kid's display?"

Morgan closed his eyes and shook his head. "That woman. She's too bloody clever for me."

"Aren't they all." Callum agreed, nodding his head toward Gemma. "She's got me wound around her little finger." At that moment Gemma caught his eye and winked at him and gave him what could only be called a sexy smile. He sighed. "And I wouldn't have it any other way."

Callum began to walk off when he stopped abruptly and turned. "Hang on a minute. Who told you about the loose hay?"

"Gemma. Who told you?"

"Rebecca."

Together they turned to the two women who, oblivious to their stares, were playing with Joe and Gemma's baby.

There was an awkward silence.

"Well," said Callum. "See you around, mate."

"Yep."

Morgan watched Callum walk away. There went his half-brother. *His*. The thought warmed him and instantly replaced the anger he'd been nurturing over the past few days as if that anger had never existed. *He had family*.

It was dark now and Rebecca didn't hear Morgan approach. She'd been standing on the veranda with Gemma who'd disappeared inside with Violet. She hadn't caught sight of Morgan for a while and her agitation grew with each passing minute. The last of the daylight had disappeared over the frozen white lake. Fairy lights dotted the huge dark trees above, casting a surreal glow on the kids who continued to play by the lake.

She turned suddenly to find him standing there watching her. "Rebecca, I—"

"Morgan! I was joking about James. I was just angry. I was stupid. Don't think I like him because I don't." She shrugged. "I mean I like him, but..." She looked helplessly at him.

"It's okay. I understand."

She looked up into his eyes and suddenly felt tears prick hers at the thought she might have risked her future with this man, who stood like a god before her—so solid, reassuring, so... *hers*. "I'm sorry..."

She didn't think he'd see in the dark of the night, but the track of her tears must have been caught by the moonlight because he raised his hands to her face and swept his thumb across her cheeks, wiping away the tears.

"You've nothing to be sorry about. It's me. I've done things all wrong. I never meant for you to find out from anyone else. It was just the way it worked out. I had to secure the land first. I couldn't come to you with nothing."

"I don't *care* about the land."

"But *I* care about *you*, which means I care about your future." His face was in shadow but she could feel the tension in his hands as his fingers thrust into her hair and held her more tightly. "I love you, Rebecca. I love everything about you." He kissed her forehead, both cheeks and her lips. He closed his eyes and placed his forehead against hers. "I can't imagine a life without you."

The tears came again then, mingling with laughter before the laughter turned to moans as they kissed again. He held her tight against him—their bodies melded against each other's, her cheek against his chest, his arms holding her close—as their breathing returned to normal. She looked up at him. "Where are you staying tonight?"

"I've a room booked at the motel."

"Do you want company? Of the female kind?"

"Sure do." He smiled. "Although I think we should hang around for a bit longer yet."

"Why?" He looked over to Joe who now ventured occasionally onto the ice under the watchful eye of Lily who was bossily giving him lessons, despite the fact that she was a few months younger than Joe. Morgan smiled and in that smile Rebecca suddenly saw what she'd failed to see before, a contentment that had been missing from him before. He turned back to her and smiled.

"I wouldn't want to interrupt Joe's big moment when he shows off the thing he made for the kids' competition." He glanced at her. "Looking forward to that." She suddenly remembered the excuse she'd made to get Morgan here in the first place.

"Um, well I think maybe that's been cancelled."

He laughed loudly and casually caressed her neck and hair before dropping his arm again. "You're a terrible liar, Rebecca."

She grinned. "I know. I did it for you, you know."

"I know you did. Thank you." He dropped a kiss on her lips and she lifted her face to his. He kissed her again, this time lingering.

"Um," he said pulling her to his side.

"Um, yourself. You're so warm." She shivered in his arms. "So... do you have a question you want to ask me?"

"If I had, I've forgotten what it was, with you looking like that." He caught her hand and pushed his fingers through hers, closing his hands around hers and pulling her to him. He dipped his head to hers. "You could make a man forget his own name," he whispered, his lips brushing her ear. He watched with satisfaction as her flesh goosebumped under his breath. She stepped closer until her breasts brushed his body. He leaned over once more. "Have you any idea what I want to do to you?"

She drew in a sharp breath, looked up at him and nodded. "Oh, yes." She licked her lips.

"And you're okay with all that now?"

She nodded. "There can't be anything wrong with the passion we have for each other. I feel safe when I'm with you, safe to be me."

"Good."

"And have you any idea what I want to do to you?"

She nodded. She certainly did. She knew exactly what he wanted to do to her.

Suddenly a gunshot went off. Morgan glanced up. "It'll be the gamekeeper shooting duck. He said he was going after a couple and must have caught their last flight."

"I doubt I'll ever get used to gunshots like you country people do."

Morgan looked back to where they'd last seen Joe. "Where's Joe?"

"Isn't he with the other kids?"

"Doesn't look like it. I think they've all just left."

They walked quickly down to where Lily was playing with Cassandra and Gemma. "Have you seen Joe?" asked Rebecca, unable to keep the sense of panic from her voice.

Rebecca glanced at Morgan who was pacing around the shores of the lake, checking the ice to see if it was broken.

"Lily," called Cassandra. "Have you seen Joe?"

"Yeah. He went running off. I don't know. Up there somewhere." She pointed toward the barn where Morgan had just been.

"Those hay bales." Morgan looked at Lily. "Why did he go running off? Any idea?"

"Those gun shots, I think. He looked frightened. I told him not to be, but I don't think he heard me." Lily shrugged.

Rebecca felt sick and for one long moment no one moved, as they all experienced the shock of realizing that Joe had walked away, off into the night and they had no idea where the troubled little boy was going or what he was going to do.

"The barn!" said Morgan. "It must have been those shots from the hunting party that did it."

Torch lights were flicked on and Rebecca watched Morgan, Callum, and other men race up to the barn. She stayed behind.

"Joe," she called, joining echoes of his name from all around. Something was wrong. She looked around at the ice, still brightly lit. She couldn't see any obvious signs of the ice breaking up. Still you couldn't be sure. She walked quickly around the edge of the lake. Gemma ran and joined her.

"You don't think he..."

"I don't know. But he can't have just disappeared into thin air. We were all at the house and he didn't go there. So he must be out here somewhere. He'll freeze unless he comes in soon."

"But surely he will."

"We discovered something the other day. Morgan and me. Putting two and two together, we think that Joe may have witnessed something, something which frightened him very much. Something to do with guns."

"Oh, no. Poor kid." Gemma called his name again and they both waited, looking around the brightly lit lake and out into the darkness. "Let's separate. I'll go and check the far side of the lake and you check to see if he's in one of the outbuildings around the house. The men will cover the other danger spots."

As Rebecca walked quickly up to the homestead, past the barn converted into Gemma's art studio, she stopped as she listened to Morgan calling his son's name. Her heart ached for him. She could hear the pain and anguish increasing with each shout.

She looked the other way to see Callum on horseback checking further afield. And then to Gemma who stood on the veranda, cuddling her baby. They exchanged worried glances. And then Gemma put her baby in her front pack and walked around the rear of the homestead to where a hill rose. No doubt to check it out a second time.

Rebecca turned full circle, trying to put herself in the mind of the troubled child she'd grown to love like he was her own. She looked around her slowly, taking in the spots where people were looking and where they weren't. It was very quiet around the courtyard, close to the house. She shone the light from her phone into the darker corners and it was then that she saw her.

Annie. Morgan's dog. Lying low under one of the large spreading trees. Rebecca frowned. She'd never known Morgan's dog to be away from Morgan's side if she could help it. But it wasn't only that. The dog's ears were pricked and her eyes were soulful. As if she was standing guard.

Rebecca looked for Morgan but he'd disappeared, his calls growing ever more distant as he widened his search. Rebecca walked over to the tree under which the dog lay and petted her head. The dog whimpered slightly. Rebecca looked around. There was nowhere for a boy to hide. It was almost completely dark now. Morgan must be going out of his mind with worry. The stars were bright tonight though. So that would help the search.

Then she heard another whimper. She looked at the dog and the dog looked back as if to say, "It wasn't me". Then something made her look up as a few flakes of snow fell from the bough of the tree. Except it wasn't snowing.

She shone the light onto a wooden ladder and saw that the ice had been disturbed. Recently scuffed.

"Joe," she called softly.

She heard another whimper and she took a deep breath and gingerly climbed up the ladder. She pushed open the hinged door and there, in the corner, was the faint shadow of a boy curled into a ball, crying softly.

She gasped with relief. Her first instinct was to stand and shout to everyone that she'd found him but she stopped herself in time. It might be her first instinct, but her first duty was to Joe.

"Hey," she said softly. "Can I join you?"

He didn't respond, simply continued to whimper, his fear revealed in the big eyes that gazed wordlessly at her.

Rebecca crawled across the icy wooden platform towards him and sat back, trying to control her shivers. She turned to him and he met her gaze with an unblinking one of his own.

"You don't mind me being here?"

She caught a slight shake of the head.

"Thanks for letting me share your space. It feels good up here." She peered down through the small window, to the ground so far beneath them and did her best to repress a shudder. "Kind of safe. Like nothing can get us."

The whimpering was interrupted by a shuddering sigh.

"I can imagine people below us putting everything away for the night, going about their business and not even knowing we were here." She smiled at him. "We could hear what they were saying, know what they were doing, but they wouldn't know anything about us."

She sat in silence for a few moments. "I guess that's all right for a while but I think I'd miss seeing things with my own eyes. Only hearing other people move around wouldn't be enough for me."

She let the silence settle for what felt like an age, listening to the little boy's breathing quietly settle.

"Do you know what I'd miss seeing?"

Joe shook his head.

"I'd miss seeing the stars."

"Why?" His first whispered word made her catch her breath.

"Because ever since I was a little girl they made me feel good."

She hadn't taken her eyes off him since he'd uttered his first word. He nodded. "They make me feel good too."

"I'd look at them and feel excited about all that wasn't known and how I couldn't wait to understand it."

He cleared his throat and wriggled a little. "I look at them and make shapes and pretend they're magic."

Her breath squeezed inside and she blinked hard but didn't look away. "Your daddy once told me that he did exactly the same thing. He used to see *taniwhas*."

Joe's eyes widened. "Did he?"

"Uh-huh," she nodded. "Shall we crawl carefully to the window and see if can see the stars? I might just get Annie to go and tell your daddy to join us, if that's okay with you."

"Yes." Joe didn't hesitate. "I wonder if he sees the same things as me in the stars."

Rebecca rolled onto her stomach and wriggled to the top of the ladder. She whistled lightly and Annie lifted her head and looked at her. "Go fetch your master," she called. "Off you go. Go fetch Morgan." The dog jumped up and ran off. For a moment Rebecca wondered if her words would have the desired effect. But you didn't have to say anything much to get Annie to join her master. She'd only been here to protect Joe as if he were a lost sheep, and now she'd been relieved of that duty, she'd head off back to where she belonged.

"Hey," she grinned at him as she crawled back in. "I've found some sleeping bags. Here." She passed him one and he pulled it around him. She did the same and they both poked their heads out of the window and looked out into the star-studded sky.

The whole world looked different under that beautiful light. And for the first time in a long time Rebecca looked at the stars, at the world, in a different way.

"You're right, it *is* magic." The light blurred a little and then came clear again. She raised her hand and pointed directly overhead to the center of the Milky Way. "Look there's the constellation of Sagittarius."

"Sagi what?"

"Sagittarius." She pointed out the pattern of stars that made up the constellation.

"It looks like a teapot."

He was right, but she'd let him explain it to her. "A teapot?"

"Yeah," he pointed, his finger describing the outline of a teapot. "And you see that end one, there?"

"Alnasl."

"Well above that are the little puffs of steam coming from the teapot."

"Oh yes. They're actually some dense matter in the Milky Way."

"The Milky Way?"

"Yes, that's the name of the galaxy of which Earth is a part."

"Oh."

Silence settled on them. A silence which Rebecca didn't want to break. For a while she thought she'd said the wrong thing. That she'd destroyed Joe's magic. She gnawed her lip. She was rubbish at this sort of thing—useless with children, hadn't the first idea of how to handle them, let alone how to heal them.

"What other shapes can you see?"

"There's a dog's head up there." Joe pointed.

"Yes. Sirius. And he's surrounded by some smaller dogs." She pointed. "See there? That's Procyon."

Joe smiled. "Oh, yeah."

Silence fell and Rebecca's mind drifted back to her childhood, to the loneliness. "You know, it wasn't just the knowledge that I thought of when I looked up at the stars."

"Did you see magic too?"

"Not so much. I used to see shapes. I used to draw the shapes that I learned about in mathematics. I'd see how many sided shapes I could draw."

"Patterns then?"

"Yes, I guess. Patterns. My magic was in patterns and shapes. Trying to bring all the stars into some kind of order so I could understand them."

"I don't think I'd want to do that."

"You don't need to. You understand them much better than I ever did. Or do." She swallowed back the sadness at her realization that, as a little girl, she'd tried to cover her loneliness and fears with an order straight from the stars. Only thing was, she hadn't healed herself, only masked her fears, covered them up and tried not to look at them again.

But she felt different now and realized she could cope with a certain amount of chaos in the stars because she felt more secure in herself. She could look at the chaos and not feel vulnerable.

"What do you mean? You're a grown up."

"You see the magic. That's the important thing."

There was a bark from below and Annie trotted up to the foot of the tree. She looked around and saw the large shadow of Morgan following her.

"Rebecca, Joe," he greeted them casually. "You both okay?"

"Sure," they replied in unison.

"Why don't you join us?" Rebecca asked.

"Right," said Morgan as he looked doubtfully at the ladder. He gripped it and then climbed carefully to the top. He shuffled next to Joe. "What are we looking at?"

"We're looking at magic, Dad," said Joe excitedly. "Rebecca's been telling me all about the magic in the stars."

"That sounds pretty cool," said Morgan, glancing over Joe's head at Rebecca.

Rebecca sat back on her heels, relieved. Joe had somehow assimilated her science with his magic to come up with his own brand of magic.

She thought of the differences between her parents and herself. And then she thought of the many differences between her and Morgan. So many differences and none of them mattered. Just because her parents had never expressed their love for her didn't mean it didn't exist. She remembered all of the little things they'd done to help her achieve her dreams and she made a mental note to return home soon to visit them. And Joe and Morgan would come with her.

Suddenly she felt Morgan's hand, reaching behind Joe's

head and finding her shoulder. She kissed it and brushed her cheek against it.

Morgan cleared his throat. "You know, Joe, when I was young I reckoned I could see a *taniwha* in those stars."

Joe and Rebecca looked at each other and laughed and kept on laughing, even while Morgan stopped looking at the stars and sat back and watched them instead. Joe curled into a ball and laughed so hard that he held onto his stomach. His joyful, infectious laugh released the tension and Rebecca and Morgan joined in as the stress left them and drifted away, up to the stars.

CHAPTER TWELVE

Rebecca looked up from her hot chocolate as Morgan walked into the kitchen at Glencoe. "Is he asleep?"

"Yeah. It didn't take him long. He was shattered after all he's been through." He patted his shirt pocket. "I've brought the baby monitor Gemma lent me, just in case he has one of his nightmares." Morgan pulled up a chair at the table and sat down. "I should have thought about the guns. Stupid of me."

"You can't think of everything. You look exhausted." Rebecca went to the fridge. "Hot chocolate?"

Morgan looked at her as if she'd gone crazy. "No way." He rose and took a bottle of whiskey from the drinks cabinet and poured himself a big shot. "Reckon my new half-brother won't mind if I indulge."

Rebecca smiled and sat down. "Reckon you're right. Reckon your new half-brother would do anything for you right now. Gemma says he feels pretty guilty about how he behaved."

Morgan took a slug of whiskey and winced slightly as

the fiery alcohol tracked down his body. "Neither of us came out of that well."

"That's family for you."

Morgan nodded and looked uncharacteristically thoughtful as he nursed his whiskey.

"Don't worry about Joe," said Rebecca, misunderstanding his silence. "He's talking to us now, we've found out what the issues are and so now we can get help for him."

Morgan looked up at her with a complex expression in his eyes.

"What is it?"

"You keep saying 'we'."

"Oh," said Rebecca, embarrassed. "I'm sorry. It's just—"

"No, don't apologize. I like it."

"You do?"

"Yeah," he said slowly. "Reckon I do."

He got up from the table and stood with his back to the open fire, looking at her with dark eyes, illuminated by the red glow of the fire. His broad chest rose and fell in a deep sigh before he took another mouthful of whiskey. Then he tilted back his head, closed his eyes and sighed again.

"You should go to bed."

He looked back at her again, his eyes hot with desire. "Yes, I should. But not without you."

She swallowed and he walked over to her and extended his hand to hers. The look, the words, the strength of his hand as he took hers, sent shock waves of desire flashing through her body. She tried to breathe evenly but failed. She opened her mouth to speak but her mouth was dry with longing and her gaze fell to his lips. His fingers curled around hers and before she knew it she was standing.

"Now, are you coming to bed or am I going to have to put you over my shoulder and carry you there?"

"Put me over your shoulder," she repeated faintly, as her imagination ran riot.

"Right then."

Before she could explain he'd scooped her up as if she weighed less than a small bale of hay, and put her over his shoulder, one hand firmly over her thighs while he finished off his whiskey.

She squealed. "Morgan West! Put me down, I was only repeating what you said. I didn't think you'd do it."

"I'm a literal man, Rebecca. You should know that by now." With the empty whiskey glass now placed on the table he ran his free hand over her bottom.

"Oh, Morgan..." She moaned and stopped wriggling, her whole attention focused on the path his fingers were taking.

He stopped abruptly. "Hold that thought." He pushed the door open suddenly, stepped out into the hall way and nearly bumped into Callum.

"Night, Morgan," Callum said calmly, as if he regularly witnessed Morgan walking off to bed with Rebecca over his shoulder. A deep blush bloomed on Rebecca's cheeks but Morgan didn't set her on her feet, instead he continued toward the staircase.

"Night, Callum."

"Sleep well, Rebecca."

Rebecca could hear the laughter in Callum's voice. "Goodnight." She lifted up a red face to see Callum disappear into the kitchen and close the door behind him. "Oh, Morgan," she said. "What's Callum going to think?"

"That we're about to have sex, I should imagine."

"Oh my," she replied faintly, as Morgan continued upstairs as if nothing had happened. Once at the top of the sweeping staircase, he walked purposefully past his own door. "Which guest room is yours?"

"The one at the end."

The old-fashioned brass door handle rattled as he twisted it and swept open the door. Her blush deepened as she thought how anyone along the corridor must have heard his heavy tread, their voices and the opening of her door. It seemed Morgan really didn't mind who knew about them. The thought made her happy.

They entered the room and she pushed the door shut with her hand. He walked up to the bed and then released his grip on her and she slid down his body and came to rest on her feet. She looked up at him and he looked down at her, not with tenderness, not with respect or deference, but with a sense of total control that made her legs weak.

"Better undress now," he said, standing back from her with folded arms.

"Morgan? What are you doing?"

"I'm making demands on you. Just like you dream of."

"But they were just daydreams, just, well, fantasies."

"Darling, I'm here to make those fantasies come true. So stop talking and take off your clothes. And pass me that scarf of yours, because we're going to need it."

It wasn't until much later that Rebecca slipped her hands free from the knots of the scarf which Morgan had deftly tied to the old-fashioned brass bed head. He'd tied them in a very loose knot. She hadn't noticed before because she hadn't wanted to move them. But now that she did, she could.

She smiled. He'd given her what she wanted but on his terms. There was no way that Morgan would ever do anything to anyone that was cruel or unkind. She curled into his warm body and he brought his arm around her, keeping her close. She sighed and went to sleep.

She awoke with her body still curled around his, her leg over his, his arm still holding her in place. She knew he was awake even without the evidence of his steady heartbeat and regular breathing.

She shifted slightly and he trailed his fingers lazily down her back. She shivered and he pulled the duvet higher over her, leaving his own body exposed. She kissed his chest and rested her cheek against it, rubbing it against the springy hair, breathing him in, wanting to hold him deep within her in any way she could.

He stroked her hair and kissed the top of his head. "I need to go back to my room. He glanced at the child monitor which had been silent all night. "I don't want Joe to wake and not find me there."

"Sure." She felt a stab of regret but knew he was right. But she couldn't resist tempting him. As he pulled away she swept her long hair over his chest, stomach and lower. Goosebumps bloomed along the trail of sensation her hair had left. And that wasn't the only thing.

She smiled sweetly. "Off you go, then." Her smile turned into a laugh as his eyes narrowed and he reached out for her. But she was too quick and sprang off the bed with a yelp. But he followed. Barefoot, she felt the difference between his height and strength to her own more keenly. Knowing how easy it would be for him to overpower her, knowing all he could do to her if he had a mind, intensified her arousal. She shivered, but not with cold, and backed up against the door.

"You going somewhere, Princess?" he asked, with raised eyebrows and no smile.

"Uh-uh." She shook her head.

"Good." He pressed his hands either side of her and she knew she was going to get more than she bargained for... and she couldn't wait.

Rebecca watched him as he got dressed. She loved watching him. He did everything with such purpose and economy. He was so *sure*. She sighed and looked out the un-curtained window. The stars were less bright now as morning approached. It had always made her a little sad, watching the stars fade from the sky. And she felt a little like that now. Even though Morgan had told her he loved her yesterday and sort of proposed to her, he'd not spoken another word about his feelings or their future together since. Seems there were drawbacks to the strong silent type.

She turned to look at him again as he collected his things and shoved them in his pocket, watching what he was doing, not her. Irrationally, she wanted him to look at her, she wanted to know what he was thinking, what he was feeling about her. He was so self-contained.

"Are you staying at Glencoe tonight?"

He shrugged. "I'm going to see how Joe is. If he's okay, we'll move into town. And after that I've made plans for us."

She brought her knees up to her chin and put her arms around her legs. "Oh." She hoped the 'us' included her but couldn't bring herself to ask. "Oh," she repeated. "What kind of plans?"

"What are you doing later on?"

"Nothing much. Why?"

"I'll show you what I have in mind."

"For you and Joe?"

Did she imagine it or was there a twinkle in his eye? "Yes." He glanced at the child monitor. "Look, I have to go now, but I'll see you later."

He closed the door with no further ado and she just sat looking at it. He was impossible! Then she flung herself back onto the pillows.

By the time Rebecca had showered and dressed Morgan and Joe had left Glencoe. And so she'd taken her time leaving Glencoe. She'd insisted on helping Gemma do her chores and spent time with baby Violet. And then by lunch time, when Morgan and Joe still hadn't returned, she decided to return to her own home. Maybe he'd meant that he'd catch up at her home, rather than Glencoe.

"I'd better go." But she didn't get up, still sat watching Gemma make some final brush strokes to her current painting.

Gemma gave Rebecca a swift assessing look before returning to her painting. "Sure." Gemma squirted some more paint onto her palette and began to mix it carefully with another color. Only then did she break the silence. "I asked Callum, but he didn't know where Morgan had gone. After what happened yesterday, maybe he's taken Joe to see someone. Was there no reply to your texts?"

"No. He's hopeless with his phone. It's always slipping under the seats in his ute, or under the bed, or"—she sighed—"or he just doesn't want to answer me." Gemma's look of sympathy was enough to make Rebecca jump up from the settee. She gave her a big hug. "Thanks for everything," she said too brightly. "It's been quite a few days!"

"Becks! Stay a little longer, I'm sure—"

"No! Honestly, I have to get back." She backed out of the studio. "Your painting is beautiful, by the way. You've caught Callum exactly, and you, and Violet..."

Gemma looked back at the painting and, with her attention once more absorbed in her painting, Rebecca slipped away.

She was glad it was the weekend and she didn't have to head off to work. She was having enough trouble focusing on everyday life, let alone her research.

She threw another log onto the fire, and curled up once more in the old, comfy armchair and tried to concentrate on the academic text she was writing. But as she tried to focus on the data she'd gathered on star formation efficiency, her mind slipped back to Morgan.

She sighed and slid her laptop onto the coffee table.

Was Morgan avoiding her? Did he regret telling her that he loved her? Were the plans he'd alluded to earlier only for him and Joe?

She picked up her phone again, willing it to ring, but unable to pluck up the courage to press the button that would make his phone ring. She didn't want to be another woman from whom he dreaded receiving phone calls.

She sat back and closed her eyes, lulled by the warmth of the fire and exhausted from a sleepless night.

She was soon asleep and her dreams were no better than her reality. She was running toward someone in a crowded space, someone who looked like Morgan. She reached him and he turned around but it wasn't Morgan. It was a stranger. Just some stranger she didn't know. She backed away and then heard a loud bang. In her dream it was gunshot and ducks flew up high in the sky, over a tree-house where a little boy looked out, fearfully. Then the sound came again but the boy disappeared. She tried to cry out, to reassure him but she couldn't seem to make a sound.

"Rebecca?"

She opened her eyes to see Morgan looking down at her.

She scrambled to her feet, getting caught in the mohair blanket that she'd been curled up in. "Morgan! What? How did you get in here?"

"I banged on the door but you didn't come, so I came around the back and saw you asleep. Are you okay? Sounded like you were having a nightmare."

"Yes." She pushed her hands through her hair. "Probably. It doesn't matter." She drew in a shaky breath and caught his gaze and held it, as a rush of anger came back to her. "Where have you been?"

He shrugged. "Why? What's the matter?"

She shook her head. "Nothing, I'm sorry. I'm being silly. It's just that I thought... it's just that I wondered if you..." She couldn't bring herself to tell him what was really on her mind. That she was scared that now she'd decided her future was with him, that he'd changed his mind.

He frowned. "I've been busy—"

"Too busy to call me? Too busy to leave a message? Must have been something important to make you that busy."

"Yes, it was," he said quietly.

"Oh..." His reply pricked the bubble of her anger and it dissolved instantly.

"I took Joe to see someone, someone who can help him. And I did some business at the same time."

"Business?"

"Yes."

"What kind?"

He walked over to the coat stand, unhooked her coat and held it out for her to take. "Put on your coat and I'll show you."

It was a half-hour ride out of Shelter Springs and late afternoon by the time Morgan pulled off the road and drove up a rough track and stopped on a ridge.

He got out the ute and Rebecca followed him. There was the scent of spring in the air.

"I remember this place. This is where we rode to."

"That's right. It's quicker by horse but I thought you might not be so keen a second time."

She looked up at him and grinned. "Good thinking." She took a deep breath of the still cold air, now edged with a hint of sweetness. "It's so beautiful up here."

"Sure is. I brought Joe here earlier and we decided where the house is going to go."

She frowned. "The house? What house? What are you talking about?"

"A house." He pointed. "Over there, just below the ridge. High enough to get all day sun, but it'll be sheltered from the southerly by the ridge behind." He smiled and she melted under its warmth. His smile seemed sunnier, more satisfied than any she'd seen before. "It'll have a fierce view. All the way down the valley, to the lake."

"You are going to build a house here."

He glanced at her with a smug, self-satisfied expression. "I thought you'd be a bit quicker on the uptake than that, Dr Mayhew, with you being so clever and all."

She narrowed her eyes in mock anger. "I'll have you

know, Mr. West, that to arrive at a hypothesis one needs to have a set of related circumstances in the first place. The only connection that I know you have to this land is that we rode out here months ago."

"It was then that I decided I wanted this land." He sighed and didn't say anything further. She knew by now that there was no way to make him speak before he was ready. She resolved to count to ten. In the end it took fifteen counts before he continued. "It was the way it lay—I knew it would be good, self-contained land for growing feed to sell and big enough to keep a viable flock of merino. It's useful to Glencoe but I could make it a lot more profitable than it currently is. I knew it'd be the perfect piece of leasehold land."

"Callum's given you the leasehold?"

"Callum's *sold* me the leasehold."

"Sold? You don't have any money!"

"As it happens, I do. My mother was paid off. I thought it was by Sir Hugh but it turns out it was Lady Mackenzie. For years Mum wasn't able to access it. But when we got out of the bush she invested the money in some commercial property in Hokitika. I never wanted a penny from it. Until now. Until I decided that it was time for me and Joe to make a home here."

Until that moment, Rebecca hadn't realized quite how much she'd been hoping the "our" in "our house" included her. She turned away and bit her lip. The wind was brisk but she looked up into the bright valley until her eyes watered. She didn't need to count the seconds now. She had no words for a moment like this.

"You're not saying anything." His voice was nearer. He'd moved closer to her but she didn't turn around. "What do you think?"

She swallowed hard and balled her hands in her pockets. She cleared her throat. "What do I think?" She gestured jerkily. "With all this? I think it's great. It's near enough to Shelter Springs for you to make sure Joe makes lots of friends at school, that he doesn't miss out on anything. And you've got the land that you've always loved. And no doubt you'll have the animals that Joe loves as well." She screwed up her eyes, willing herself to focus on Morgan's future, on Joe's future, but *not* her future. Then she took in another long slow breath and turned to face him. "I think you'll both be very happy here."

She was surprised to see his face solemn. He looked away abruptly. "Is that all you can say?"

"What do you want me to say?"

"I know you think we're total opposites and I'm not denying that. But"—he turned to her and the anguish in his face nearly undid her—"but, you know, it's not *how* we look at things, it's *the things* we look at."

"What do you mean?"

"Okay." He thought for a few moments. If she'd been counting now, she'd have lost count. "When we look at the stars, you see these"—he waved his hand in a vaguely geometric pattern—"triangles and squares and patterns that try to turn your universe into some nice ordered thing and all I see is"—he gestured helplessly—"*taniwhas*." She failed to smother a laugh and before she could draw breath he'd taken her in his arms. "But, Rebecca, we're both looking at the stars and seeing our own kind of magic. It doesn't matter *how* we look at things, it's that we both *want* the same things out of life. And we do. I've seen you with Joe. You're kind, you're curious about life, you're *full* of life. You've lived all over the world but it's this place that called to you, this place where you chose to make your home."

She swallowed. It was the most she'd ever heard him say in one go. "You're right. I knew it as soon as I came here that I never wanted to leave. And you did, too, didn't you? You avoided it all your life but now you're here, you can't leave it. It's your home. It's in your blood."

He nodded, his forehead pressed now against hers. "Say you'll make this home, yours too?"

She gulped as she tried to contain her emotions. He mistook the pause.

"Rebecca! What do I have to do to persuade you to live here with me?"

She half-laughed, half cried. "You can't."

"Why not?"

"Because you don't have to persuade me to do anything. You're right. We both see the beauty in the world. And between my shapes and your *taniwhas* I reckon we can sort things out. Morgan, I love you and I want to marry you. Will you marry me?"

"Rebecca..." He caressed her chin, her lips and kissed her closed eyelids. "I thought you'd never ask."

EPILOGUE

Eighteen months later...

S ummer seemed to be lasting forever in the Mackenzie country and Rebecca was thankful that Morgan had the foresight to insist on the wrap-around veranda onto which all the rooms opened out. She sat back on one of the cushioned chairs grouped on the veranda to make the most of the view and the cooling breezes, and drank from a long glass of cold mint tea.

She picked up an old diary from the top of a pile of books and papers she'd been sorting through and fanned herself with it, shifting her swollen belly into a more comfortable position as she did so.

It was past five in the afternoon and Morgan and Joe had just left the newly built barn and were returning to the homestead through the grass that grew all around them like a sea of gold.

Joe had shot up in the past eighteen months. It was clear he was going to be as tall as Morgan, if not taller. But that wasn't the only way in which he'd changed.

There were no more nightmares, no more being startled at the sound of gunshot, no more long silences. She smiled to herself as his freckled face turned up to talk to Morgan who listened but obviously didn't see the need to reply beyond the occasional affirmative grunt.

Joe ran up the steps onto the veranda and plonked himself in the chair beside Rebecca.

"Hey!" he greeted her.

"There's some home-made lemonade in the fridge." He jumped up. "And some baking on the bench."

"Cool."

As Joe disappeared inside, Rebecca shouted out after him. "And bring some out for your dad."

"You spoil that boy," said Morgan coming to halt before her. He dropped his hat onto the table and stood, hands on hips, looking her over. It never ceased to have an effect on her. "You shouldn't be baking in this heat. You remember what the doctor said... rest."

She waved her hand. "Oh, I'm fine. Don't fuss. It's just a baby." She patted her stomach, her finger lingering as she met his heated gaze.

He placed his hand over hers and smoothed it gently around her stomach. "Not *just* anything. He's our son. Joe's brother."

"And my little scientist." She grinned.

He dipped his head and kissed her just as Joe appeared balancing a jug of lemonade, some glasses and a plate of scones, munching as he came.

"I don't understand why you want a scientist when you've Dad and me," Joe said with a mouthful of scone. "Eh, Dad?"

"That's right. What more could she want with two big guys like us around?"

She shrugged. "It's true. But you have to face the possibility that your new brother might go around making lists like I do and he might, just *might* see using a computer as fun, rather than a punishment."

Joe rolled his eyes. "No more lists!"

Rebecca laughed. "Joseph West, you'll just have to get used to me and my lists. We go together."

Joe bobbed to the ground and picked up a stray piece of paper. "Like this one?" He waved it in the air.

Rebecca colored, immediately recognizing it. It must have fallen out of her old diary that she'd picked up to fan herself. She reached out for it. "Hey, Joe, that's mine."

Joe read the piece of paper out loud. "There's a lot of scribble on this list. But I can just about read what's under it. Number one...must be self confi...confi—I can't read the rest and number two, must be 're-something' of women, I think it says. And then some crossings out. Number five is 'Tall' and then more crossings out and the word 'clever' is written in." He looked up at her, frowning. "This is a strange list. What is it?"

Morgan grinned, plucked it from his son's hands and gave it back to Rebecca. "Some daft fancy of your mother's."

Rebecca took it from Morgan with an embarrassed glare. "Sometimes one has to write a list simply to know that it's the wrong list."

"What?" Joe exclaimed. "I don't get it."

"It's understandable." She sighed. "I'm not sure I do."

"So why was everything crossed out and only your name written at the end, Dad?"

Rebecca blushed and folded the list over and over in her hands. But Morgan just kept looking at her. "Just my name, eh Rebecca?"

"Sometimes all you need is one name. Sometimes you don't need anything else to describe what you want."

"I don't know what you're all talking about," said Joe as he took the opportunity of his mum and dad's diverted attention to stuff another scone into his mouth, while pocketing a third. He stood up and whistled, and a small sheepdog jumped up from beside Annie who lay, one eye open, in the shade. He reached down and petted her. "Good girl. Sasha and I are going to check on the horses, Dad. I'll take Neptune out for a ride to the end paddock and back."

"That's fine, lad. Take your time."

"Okay."

They heard Joe walk away whistling. The atmosphere seemed to thicken and become airless as Morgan reached down and grabbed her hands and pulled her to standing.

"Because *sometimes* what you want has been staring you in the face all along." He kissed her gently on the lips. "Isn't that right, Mrs West?"

She smiled as he pulled her inside the house. "It certainly is, Mr. West."

AFTERWORD

Thank you for reading *What you See in the Stars*. I hope you enjoyed it! *What you See in the Stars* is the fourth book in The Mackenzies series. An excerpt follows of the next book in the series—*Second Chance at Whisper Creek*—which features James and Susie. The Mackenzies series consists of:

A Place Called Home (Guy and Lucia)
Secrets at Parata Bay (Dallas and Cassandra)
Escape to Shelter Springs (Callum and Gemma)
What you See in the Stars (Morgan and Rebecca)
Second Chance at Whisper Creek (James and Susie)
Summer at the Lakehouse Café (Pete and Lizzi)

Happy reading!

Sophie

SECOND CHANCE AT WHISPER CREEK

BOOK 5 OF THE MACKENZIES—JAMES

A woman who values her independence. A playboy who wants to make amends for past mistakes. A trust that has to be earned...

James Mackenzie is tired of his shallow lifestyle and wants a

*family. But before he begins his new life he needs to salve his
conscience by making sure the future is secure for the woman
he wronged ten years earlier.*

*The last thing Susie Henderson needs is her ex buying the
winery in which she works and threatening her independence. She's worked hard to get where she is and she has no
intention of making herself vulnerable again.*

*But the deep love and affection they felt for each other hasn't
gone away. So Susie has to figure out how to trust someone
who betrayed her, someone who has lost his way and no
longer believes in himself...*

Excerpt

"You like my mum, don't you?"

He looked around to see Tom watching him quietly.
"Sure do. Not so sure she likes me much."

"Why? What did you do?"

How like a ten-year-old to cut straight to the heart of the
matter. "I made a mistake."

"That doesn't sound so bad."

"It was a big mistake."

"Say 'sorry' then."

James nodded thoughtfully. It was true, he'd never actually apologized for his behavior. Years ago she'd disappeared
off the map. He'd waited, expecting her to return, leaving
messages wherever he thought she might be. But she hadn't
returned to Glencoe and she hadn't returned his messages.
And now? He'd somehow avoided saying the actual words.

"You know? You've got a good head on your shoulders.
I'll give it a try."

"It'll work. Mum always forgives me when I mess up, so long as I admit to it and apologize."

"Thanks for the tip, mate." He jumped up. "Come on, let's go and see what she's up to."

They found her just inside the curtain of pohutukawas, drawing water from a pump.

"A pump? I thought this bay was uninhabited."

"It is now. But years ago?" She pushed aside a curtain of creepers. "Fantastic, isn't it?"

James couldn't see what she was looking at and preferred not to shift his own view. "Breathtaking," James murmured as he focused on her long, lean, limbs. With effort, he shifted his gaze from her chest to whatever it was that was holding her attention. He walked up beside her.

She shifted the veil of vegetation further to reveal a grand, two-storied, colonial house whose white paint had peeled, leaving scars of silvered wood, some rotten. Elsewhere, curling green tendrils of creepers probed into its nooks and crannies. "Been that way for over fifty years."

"Wow. Who'd have thought this was hiding behind these trees?" He looked up at the intricately balconied widow's walk along its upper story, set amidst a crescent of flowering pohutukawa trees. "It's like something out of a fairy tale."

Tom came running up behind them. "Perhaps there's a princess inside who needs a kiss to wake her up?

Susie groped behind a ledge and produced a key. "Trust a person of the male species to believe a kiss could set everything right. When something's dead, it's dead."

James watched her walk up and take Tom's hand before opening the door. In that moment he realized just how much, and how deeply, he'd hurt her. And, for the first time, he wondered if he could ever put it right.

ALSO BY SOPHIE HAYDON

The Mackenzies

A Place Called Home

Secrets at Parata Bay

Escape to Shelter Springs

What you See in the Stars

Second Chance at Whisper Creek

Summer at the Lakehouse Café

Lantern Bay

Yours to Give

Yours to Treasure

Yours to Cherish

Yours to Keep

Yours Forever

Yours to Love

ABOUT THE AUTHOR

Hello!

My name is Sophie Haydon and I write romances with stories which make you turn the pages, and characters who feel real.

I'm an avid people watcher, hopeless romantic and dreamer who spends far too much time gazing out the window, imagining scenes where people struggle with life and emotions but always end up happily. Because, yes, I'm also an eternal optimist!

I currently have two connected series — Mackenzies and Lantern Bay — which feature the Mackenzie and Connelly families. At the moment, I'm writing the fifth Lantern Bay book, but am already planning future series.

All the books I've written so far are set in New Zealand, where I live. But I was born on the north Norfolk coast of England and am planning a series set in the small seaside town in which I grew up. And then there's my Nantucket trilogy which I began planning years ago, but have yet to find time to write.

So, wherever you are in the world, welcome to my little corner, where I sit with my two cocker spaniels snoring gently beside me, creating worlds where people struggle with life and emotions but are always rewarded with love and happiness in the end. Because that's non negotiable!

I hope you enjoy my books.

Sophie

x